It had to be a nightmare, but it felt so real...

Cord was lying naked on a metal slab in a hospital basement, unable to move. A bearded man in a white lab coat entered the room. The man was huge, his head rising nearly to the buzzing fluorescent lights on the ceiling. He was hairy, with tufts of fur curling out of the sleeves of his lab coat. Something was wrong with his eyes. One eye stared blankly ahead, the other was pure black. A scar ran across his face, from temple to cheekbone, disappearing into his beard.

The man spoke into a hand recorder: "Suspected cause of death: brain hemorrhage, autopsy pending." He picked through surgical instruments on a rollaway stand for a rusty scalpel. He raised the instrument and sank it deep into Cord's side then pulled out a handful of intestines and twisted them around his forearm, like an electrician folding a cable. He severed the intestines with an enterotome and laid them on the stand, dripping blood and gristle down onto the stainless steel table. Cord couldn't move—couldn't wake—could only watch in horror as the coroner picked up a bone saw and carved into his chest.

He pulled apart the skin and severed a few ribs with a hooked rib cutter. Blood flew up in a watery spray, spackling the coroner's lab coat.

Then he reached into Cord's chest cavity and pulled out his still-beating heart...

Dean "Corduroy" Masland is an experienced MMA cage fighter. One night during a sanctioned bout, he accidentally kills his best friend, Vic Mercy, with a second-round right hook to the temple. The next morning, Cord awakens to find a prophetic tattoo—his own name and date of death—etched into the back of his neck, dated four days in the future. Soon, he encounters a seven-foot-tall demon in a blood-speckled lab coat, bent on fulfilling the prophecy. As if things could get any worse, the police begin to suspect Vic's death wasn't an accident and peg Cord as the prime suspect. But unless he can unravel the dark magic behind his tattoo, Cord won't live long enough to clear his name. The countdown to his expiration date has officially begun...

KUDOS for *Expiration Date*

In *Expiration Date* by Scott McNeight, Cord Masland is an MMA cage fighter who kills his best friend in a match. Branded as a killer by his friend's family, even though it was an accident, Cord also wakes up the next morning with a new tattoo on the back of his neck, giving his birth date and his death date—4 days in the future. Then if that's not bad enough, a demon he calls the Coroner is after him, determined to kill him. When the police detective investigating the friend's death decides that it wasn't an accident, Cord also becomes the prime suspect. Man, he's really having a bad week! The story is a fascinating glimpse into the world of MMA cage fighting with a paranormal twist that is both chilling and intriguing. I found the book extremely hard to put down. ~ *Taylor Jones, Reviewer*

Expiration Date by Scott McNeight is a paranormal thriller. Our hero, Dean "Corduroy" Masland, is an experienced MMA cage fighter, the MMA being mixed martial arts. During one such match, Cord accidentally kills his best friend, Victor Mercy, who dies in his arms. When Cord wakes up the next morning, he discovers that he has a new tattoo on the back of his neck, one that he doesn't remember getting. This strange tattoo gives his name, his nickname, his birthdate, and lists a date of death as April 15, 2016, which is only four days away. Then Cord begins to encounter a seven-foot-demon in a blood-spattered lab coat, who Cord refers to as the Coroner.

Now Cord needs to unravel the dark magic behind his tattoo, and fast, or it won't even matter that the police think he killed Victor on purpose to avenge an old wrong. He isn't going to live long enough to have to worry about proving his innocence. *Expiration Date* is chilling and tense, combining the already-dangerous world of cage fighting with the black magic of demons and evil curses. An exciting read that will keep you turning pages from beginning to end. ~ *Regan Murphy, Reviewer*

ACKNOWLEDGEMENTS

I've got to start with Dan Pope, whose editing skills transformed this book from rough conception to publishable-quality fiction. If it weren't for Dan, I'm certain this book would never have reached print. Dan, you rock.

Many thanks to Brian Clements, who took a flyer on a quiet, literary kid from Marist and invited him to his wonderful program. The rest, as they say, is history.

To the gang at the Rez, for all the editing advice and, more importantly, for all the late nights at the Maron—which were the true inspiration.

To Lisa Siedlarz for the long phone conversations, guiding me through all the plot snags, like an experienced ship captain on the lookout for icebergs.

Gratitude to John Roche for the referral to Black Opal Books and for the knowledge that curmudgeons can still be pretty decent human beings and great friends.

To the awesome team at BOB: Faith, Jack, Elise, and Lauri for taking a chance on this book.

To Holly, for being my best friend, and for caring about this novel probably more than anyone.

To my parents for their support.

To Michelle for putting up with me all the times I had to lock myself in my writing room downstairs for days, rarely venturing out.

And thanks to my amazing son, Victor James, whose first name I borrowed for use in this book. I thought long and hard about changing the name, given the arc of Vic Mercy's narrative, but then I realized that Mercy, first-and-foremost, is a fighter, something I know my son always will be too.

EXPIRATION DATE

SCOTT MCNEIGHT

A Black Opal Books Publication

Black Opal Books

BECAUSE SOME STORIES JUST HAVE TO BE TOLD

GENRE: PARANORMAL THRILLER/ROMANTIC ELEMENTS

This is a work of fiction. Names, places, characters and incidents are either the product of the author's imagination or are used fictitiously, and any resemblance to any actual persons, living or dead, businesses, organizations, events or locales is entirely coincidental. All trademarks, service marks, registered trademarks, and registered service marks are the property of their respective owners and are used herein for identification purposes only. The publisher does not have any control over or assume any responsibility for author or third-party websites or their contents.

DEDICATION

To Victor James:
My first book for my first, and only, boy.

FOUR DAYS...

CHAPTER 1

The morning after the fight, Cord woke in pain. He couldn't see out of one eye. His head pounded. When he got out of bed, his right knee buckled. He staggered downstairs to find his housemate, Lovie, asleep on the kitchen table with a smear of jelly across his chin and a pencil lodged sideways in his mouth.

Cord pulled out a chair, upending Leonidas—Lovie's tabby. The cat swatted at him then disappeared under the table—a natural fighter, descendant of the tiger.

Lovie woke, blinking his eyes as if from a strong glare. He spat out the pencil and swung his legs off the table. "Damn that Senator. That's the second pencil this week."

"Who made this mess?"

"Dunno. I didn't recognize half of the people here. It was supposed to be a warm-up party for your event, but we never got there, you know?"

Lovie talked like a valley girl, punctuating his statements with questions, rarely finding satisfactory answers. "Your nose looks broken, pal."

"It is," Cord said.

"Sorry I missed the fight. How'd it go?"

"I fought Mercy in the prelims." Cord choked out the words in a hoarse whisper. He didn't even recognize his own voice.

Lovie whistled, a low note. "Vic Mercy is one fearsome dude. I know he's your best buddy and all, but still. That's a tough draw."

"I fought the fight of my life."

Lovie raised an eyebrow. "Yeah? You win?"

Cord's vision blurred. He took a deep breath. "I won."

Lovie fist-pumped the air, the table groaning under his weight. Then he paused. "Wait, this is a good thing, right?"

"It was a right hook, two minutes into the second round. Flush to the temple," Cord said, staring straight ahead. "I knew something was wrong, the way his knees buckled."

"You're saying what?"

"He hit the floor. I held him. Then he was dead."

"Wait, what?" said Lovie, his mouth gaped. "You killed him? Your best buddy?"

"I did." Cord could still *feel* it, the snap of the punch, the way the impact had traveled all the way up his arm, through his body. A perfect hook. With shame, he recalled the excitement he felt when the punch landed. The glee. The fucking delight. And then, a second later, as Vic fell, the regret of what he had done, the terrible, everlasting guilt already sinking in.

"Jesus, Cord." Lovie studied Cord with narrowed eyes, an expression of deep concentration. The process of thought seemed to cause him actual physical pain. "This may be a bad time, but Bookmaker had you at even odds to win your opening fight."

"So what?"

"I threw in for five hundred. That's a nice paycheck. Unless killing the other guy cancels all bets. I mean, it's still a win, technically?"

"Fuck you, Lovie." Cord shoved out of the chair and returned to his bedroom with an icepack.

෧৩෧

Cord, always small for his age, had learned to scrap as a youngster. He took karate classes at seven, lived on a diet of Bruce Lee films, classic boxing replays, and more recently, mixed martial arts pay-per-views.

A defining moment: in eighth grade, Sean Cramer, a held-back fifteen year-old, knocked a pile of books out from under his arm in the hallway. Cord imagined himself—as always—scrambling along the cracked tiles while his classmates crowed with laughter. Instead, he tried something new—a Rocky Marciano overhand right. The fist connected with Cramer's nose, pushing the cartilage to the other side of his face.

Cord got a two-day suspension, but when he returned, his classmates carried his books to study hall, chanting his name.

Cord had collected fighting memorabilia ever since his first allowance. Now, at twenty-nine, he owned a pretty decent assortment: the laces from Ted "Kid" Lewis's gloves, the loincloth worn by Kotokaze Kōki when he won the 1983 Sumo Championships in Tokyo, Ken Shamrock's blood-crusted incisor—two hundred ninety-three dollars on eBay, complete with certificate of authenticity signed by Shamrock himself—and his prized possession, Bruce Lee's fighting stick.

He rented a house in High Falls, New York, with two college buddies, Lovie and Senator. They'd graduated together from Pace University in 2008. They were good guys, but they had no respect for his memorabilia, particularly when they were intoxicated, which was most of the time. Cord worked as a gravedigger and nightshift security guard at the Woodside Cemetery near the Roosevelt Mansion, and he often came home to find his collectible wrestling figurines spread out in homoerotic poses on his bedroom floor with Hulk Hogan ass-humping The Rock. Other times he'd find a tangle of arms and legs under his sheets, usually Senator with some dude he'd met that night. Cord had installed a lock on his door, which was broken the following day. His roommates weren't much for privacy.

In nine years as an amateur fighter, Cord had broken almost as many bones as Evel Knievel: his right ankle, three or four ribs, and his left arm, which still bothered him every time it rained. He'd broken the arm in an after-hours match at an Atlantic City bar, an unlicensed under-ground event. His opponent was a two hundred sixty-five pound Norwegian with a scraggly yellow beard, six foot six, maybe six foot seven. Cord had weighed in at one-hundred-sixty-nine that night, five-foot-nine in his bare feet, three weight classes below his opponent, but this wasn't the UFC. Looking back, Cord should've taken one look at the guy and called the whole thing off, but—stupidly—he'd gone through with it.

Later, he'd blame it on dumb pride. He'd never been one to back down against stiff odds. Within a minute, the Norseman pinned him to the canvas, wrapped his legs over Cord's torso, and locked him in an arm bar. Cord tapped, but the "ref" had turned away to chat it up with a biker chick in the front row—and the Norseman kept cranking until Cord's elbow popped, the bone giving way like the snap of dry kindling.

Cord's amateur record was fourteen and eight, but he'd won and lost twenty or more unlicensed events. Many mornings, he woke bruised and battered after bar fights with little or no recollection whom he'd fought. All those injuries, all that pain, but nothing compared to this day.

The headache, the bashed ribs, broken nose—and the nightmare knowledge that he'd killed Vic Mercy, his best friend in the world since he was seven years old.

He glanced at the twenty-gallon fish tank on top of the dresser. His angelfish, Rocky, who'd been with him since his twenty-third birthday, lay belly-up among the pebbles and ferns at the bottom of the tank. Lulu, his other angelfish, nibbled at his corpse. Another casualty of the prior night.

"Jesus, Cord. I just heard." Senator stood in the doorway, wearing his black Giorgio Brutini suit, hair neatly gelled to the side. He gave Cord a hug. That was Senator's thing, hugging. Any chance he got, he'd maul you like a black lab. Partying was also his thing. Back in the day, he liked to pop Ecstasy and hit the city clubs, staggering home at dawn, looking like something you'd see in a George Romero film. At twenty-nine, he'd cut down on the raves but not the revelry. Often Cord found him naked and gyrating in front of a strobe light late at night, the psychedelic beats of electronic trance reverberating throughout the house.

When he released his grip, Cord smelled like he'd just taken a bath in Vetiver. "I'm sorry," Senator said. "It's all over the news. The blogs are calling you Killer Cord Masland."

"It feels like a bad dream."

"Why Mercy?"

"We drew each other in the first round. Simple as that." Their martial arts instructor, Sifu Lao, used to make them spar with one another. Lao believed in full-contact training, max-effort, moving targets. This, he'd felt, prepared them both for the cage *and* for real-life. *Better you bruise here now than bleed out on the street*, he said. "We'd fought plenty of times," Cord said. "Once in Union City—"

"I remember, last fall, the Union City Fi'ty."

Cord nodded. That night there'd been fifty fighters,

one "grand" prize: five-hundred bucks. He and Mercy had faced off in the semi-finals. Mercy had ended the fight by wrenching Cord's arm behind his back, forcing him to tap. "Say uncle, bitch," Mercy had hissed. Afterward, they'd spent Mercy's winnings at the bar.

"How do you remember these things?" Cord asked.

Senator shrugged. He had a great memory for random facts. He'd memorized the birthdays of all the people he knew—working PR as the son of Congressman Brady Valor, he knew a great many. He sent out prompt birthday cards, ones decorated with cupcakes that said things like, *Hope you have a super sweet day!* He addressed the cards, *Team Valor.*

"Vic broke my nose that night," Cord said. "For the first time."

"That doesn't look too good right now, either. You want to tell me what happened?"

"Well, you can guess. I caught him. Solid. After he fell, I tried to hold him up. His lips were moving. It was like he was trying to tell me something, but no words were coming out. Blood ran out of his mouth. That was the worst of it, you know? The blood." Cord paused, drawing in a shaky breath.

Senator put a hand on his shoulder. "It's okay, buddy."

"His eyes fluttered, then stayed open—like he was staring at me, but there was nothing inside. I called for a doctor, but I already knew he was gone. He died in my arms, right there on the mat."

Senator threw his arms around Cord. "Chin up," he

said. Then he drew back, his brow furrowed. "When did you get that?"

"What?"

"On your neck."

"What are you talking about?"

"The tattoo."

Cord ducked into the bathroom and angled a hand mirror so he could see into the full-length one behind. There was a fresh tattoo on the back of his neck. Crisp black edges, intricate lettering etched into his skin.

Dean "Corduroy" Masland
Born
September 7, 1986
Died
April 15, 2016

"What day is this?" he called to Senator.

"Sunday."

"No, the date."

"The eleventh," he said. "April eleventh."

Cord ran hot water in the sink and scrubbed the back of his neck. He toweled dry, checked again. The tattoo was still there, as fresh as before. Not even a smudge. So it wasn't the removable kind. He reached under the sink and pulled out the industrial soap, the gritty stuff that came in an unmarked white container with a pump on top. Lovie had brought it home from work the last time he'd had a job—middle-school janitor, 2014. Cord pumped the blue gunk onto his palm and scrubbed the back of his neck. It felt like washing with sand. When he rinsed and looked again, there was no change. The tattoo seemed more vivid, if anything.

"Seriously, dude," Senator said. "That's a creepy thing to ink onto your neck."

"I didn't do it."

"How did it get there?"

"Hell if I know."

Cord replayed the night's events. At seven, he'd met Mercy at his apartment, and together they'd driven to the Newark Prudential Center. It was the biggest event in their fighting careers. The winner would receive five thousand dollars and an invitation to FightFest, a national event in Youngstown, Ohio. Mercy had insisted on driving, saying he was too nervous to spectate in the passenger seat. Cord had been happy to oblige. He wasn't crazy about driving to unfamiliar places. They got their brackets ten minutes before the fight. *Round One: Mercy vs. Masland.*

"Looks like it's you and me, brother," Mercy had said.

At the stare-down, they bro-hugged and patted each other on the back.

During the fight, Mercy had moved well, as quick as Cord had ever seen him. He caught Cord with a stiff combination, the second punch connecting with his nose, which gave way with a sickening crunch. Cord's vision darkened, and he had instinctively thrown the right hook that ended the fight—and his friend's life.

He had spent much of the night talking to cops, getting fingerprinted like a criminal, first in Newark, then at High Falls PD, where Cord answered questions for an hour. A detective—Gallo, in his fifties, with a serious limp—jotted notes in a folder. Numb, still in shock, Cord heard his own voice as if it belonged to someone else. Finally, Gallo said, "You're free to go, Mr. Masland. Sorry to have held you up."

After they released him, he'd taken Mercy's car home, getting in at four in the morning. No visit to the tattoo parlor—not unless he did it in his sleep.

ɞɷɞɷ

That afternoon the phone rang—Brandi, his sometimes girlfriend. He hadn't seen her in a week, maybe more. He stared at the phone, imagining her nasally condolences, imagining having to explain what had happened all over again. Not that she wouldn't care—maybe she would. But he wouldn't. That was the problem with them. He liked her well enough, at least her body. But they'd been "dating" for the better part of a year, and yet, in his mind, it had never reached much past the point of casual sex.

When the phone rang again, he figured he'd have to answer this time, but it wasn't Brandi. It was Mark. Half-brother—they had the same father. "You made the front page, Dean. There's your picture in black and white—looks like a mug shot, actually. Under that, the headline: 'MMA fighter killed in cage—'"

"Actually, bro, don't read it to me."

"No?"

"I'm not up for talking about it right now."

"You must be in hell."

"You could say that."

"How did it happen?"

"I really don't want to talk about it right now." As much as Cord tried to forget about the fight, his brother's nagging voice brought it all back. That killer right hook. Vic's crumpled body lying on the canvas. Cord's best friend in the world. Dead, by Cord's own hand. It didn't seem possible, and yet he remembered every moment as if the images were seared into his memory. The pre-fight posturing, the first and second round battles. And, of course, the worst image of them all: holding Vic's broken body as his blood dripped onto the canvas.

Doctors had run into the cage then, yelling for space, and yet he'd clung to his friend's body. He couldn't let go. How stupid. What if those few moments had been critical to Vic's survival? What if he'd still had a chance to live?

"You *are* shaken up," Mark said. "I can hear it in your voice."

"Of course, I'm shaken up," Cord yelled, "my best friend just died in a fucking cage."

"I'm glad Pop's not around to witness this anger. This anger and terrible violence. It's sinful, Dean."

Cord held the phone away from his ear, strangling the receiver. Mark and his religious crap. Mark's mother and stepfather had died in a car accident when he was a teenager, and after that he'd embraced God and His divine plan. Personally, Cord didn't see anything divine about some drunk plowing through a guardrail at ninety. Mark could believe what he wanted to believe, but Cord couldn't stand to hear scripture, particularly not this morning. Cord brought the receiver back to his ear with a sigh. *He means well*, Cord thought. *At least, I think he does.*

"I stopped by Pop's grave this morning. I was disturbed by the condition of the plot."

"Call Rusty Suggs. He's the caretaker. I just dig the graves. You know that."

"Doesn't it concern you that your own *father's* headstone was vandalized?"

"What are you talking about?"

"Someone kicked over Pop's headstone."

"That's impossible. That stone weighs a ton." When Rusty had placed his father's gravestone, he'd had to hook up the trailer to a rotatable crane—the *Tank*, they called it. The headstone was solid marble, three hundred fifty pounds at least.

"I was there an hour ago. Saw it with my own eyes."

Cord frowned. As far as he knew, his brother hadn't visited the old man's grave since the funeral. His involvement in Stan's burial was solely financial—he paid for the headstone. Cord had tried to convince him to come to the graveside service. But Mark hadn't been close to his father.

In truth, Cord didn't blame Mark. Cord hadn't gotten along very well with Stan either. The old man had been a selfish prick on good days.

He called Mark a mistake, "The unwanted spawn of my loins."

"I'll deal with it when I go in tonight, okay?"

"Fine."

"'To the living we owe respect,'" Cord said, quoting Voltaire. "'To the dead we owe only truth.'"

Mark paused. "Then you owe some truth to Vic Mercy, my brother."

CHAPTER 2

Cord had a slew of tattoos. Tribal designs on his biceps, a naked lady on his back, Latin words on his forearms—*carpe diem, non omnis moriar*—a flame across his calf, an eagle arcing across the burn scar on his clavicle. And his favorite: the three Chinese symbols for Bruce Lee's Jeet Kune Do—Jie, Quan, and Dao—across his chest. Roughly translated: *The Way of the Intercepting Fist*.

All his tattoos hurt for a few days. But this new tattoo on the back of his neck didn't hurt at all. It already felt completely healed. He would never wash, scour, or even towel-dry a fresh tattoo, because the ink might run. But even after he'd used the blue gunk, the design on his neck remained flawless.

He wondered if he had a concussion as well as a broken nose. Had he blacked out a good part of the night? Stopped at an open-all-night parlor and gotten inked? But why that design? Why inscribe his alleged date of death—four days from now—onto his neck? Had the tattooist done it as some sort of sick joke?

The way he felt now, he almost welcomed death. Almost. When it came down to it, though, he wasn't ready to die. He hadn't accomplished half the things he'd wanted in life—UFC contract, wife, kids, a house big enough for an octagon cage. Hell, his twenties were just about over, and he didn't even possess things most people took for granted—a decent salary, for starters. His idea of financial security was having enough in the bank to cover rent *and* cable for the month. He used to consider grave-digging the perfect job, but he couldn't recall exactly why at the moment. Mostly, it was just backbreaking labor. Minimum wage meant one thing when you were a kid, quite another when you were pushing thirty.

He prodded the tattoo on his neck and now felt a sense of unease creep over him. What could it mean? Who did it? Senator and Lovie liked to play practical jokes on him, but not something like this. Was someone toying with him? Cord had rivals, sure, but he couldn't think of any fighter who'd want to bring that rivalry outside of the cage.

None of it made sense, and it hurt to think. His head pounding, he fell into bed, hoping for a nap before work…

࿇

He was lying naked on a metal slab in a hospital basement. A bearded man in a white lab coat entered the room. The man was huge, his head rising nearly to the buzzing fluorescent lights on the ceiling. He was hairy, with tufts of fur curling out of the sleeves of his lab coat. Something was wrong with his eyes. One had a coffee-creamer cataract, which stared blankly ahead, the other was pure black. A scar ran across his face, from temple to cheekbone, disappearing into his beard.

The man spoke into a hand recorder: "Suspected cause of death: brain hemorrhage, autopsy pending." He picked through surgical instruments on a roll-away stand for a rusty scalpel. He raised the instrument and sank it deep into Cord's side then pulled out a handful of intestines and twisted them around his forearm, like an electrician folding a cable. He severed the intestines with an enterotome and laid them on the stand, dripping blood and gristle down onto the stainless steel table. Cord couldn't move—couldn't wake—could only watch in horror as the coroner picked up a bone saw and carved into his chest.

He pulled apart the skin and severed a few ribs with a hooked rib cutter. Blood flew up in a watery spray, spackling the coroner's lab coat.

He reached into Cord's chest cavity and pulled out his still-beating heart…

ⱷↄⱷↄ

Cord opened his eyes, gasping for breath, his heart drumming inside his chest.

Senator stood in the doorway. "You okay?"

"Yeah." Cord shook his head, the dream slipping away. "Yeah, I'm okay."

"Someone's here to see you."

Cord recognized the cop. Gallo, the detective who'd taken his statement the night before. He wore a trench coat despite the mild weather, khakis, boat shoes, and a fedora askew on his head. He leaned on a cane. He took a tentative sip of Senator's coffee—an unfortunate choice, which would surely send him to the bathroom within the hour.

"Detective Gallo, CFPD."

"I remember. From last night." Cord introduced himself for no reason. "Dean Masland." The words felt foreign on his tongue, like he was trying to pass himself off as someone else. "What can I do for you, Detective?"

Gallo took off his hat, pushed a few empty beer cans out of the way on the kitchen table, and sat down. "You boys celebrate last night?"

"Not me. My roommates. They generally do that every night."

"Life's one big party for you guys, isn't it?"

"Not lately."

"I have a few follow-up questions about the mishap."

Mishap. "That right?"

"Newark didn't want to touch it, so this baby landed in my lap. I hate loose ends." Gallo pointed at a chair. "You mind sitting?"

Cord fell into a chair and crossed his legs, wincing at the tightness in his hamstrings, typical for the day after a fight.

"After talking with you last night, I got to thinking about you and the deceased. This was your best friend, right?"

"Since second grade."

"And you got into this MMA stuff together, correct?"

Cord nodded. "We trained together four times a week. We watched probably every pay-per-view ever, going back to when it was bare-knuckle. Back then, it was legal to pull hair and knee guys in the balls."

"Nice."

"Under those rules, anybody could get in the cage. Ever hear of Tank Abbott? Big beard and a beer gut? The kind of guy you'd find in a biker bar. Vic used to love watching that dude pound the snot out of someone."

Gallo took a sip of coffee, grimaced. "I did two tours in 'Nam. Seventy-one and seventy-two. For kicks, we used to set up a makeshift boxing ring in one of the tents. We had a few sets of gloves. Sergeant looked the other way, and we'd go at it. We had time on our hands." He reached for the coffee cup then thought better of it. "My buddy came from a boxing background; his father was Golden Gloves. One day we were working up a sweat while he tried to teach me the footwork. I threw a punch he wasn't expecting and caught him on the chin. It hit him just right, and he went down hard."

Cord shuddered, thinking of his right connecting with Mercy's skull. "You killed him?"

"Course not," Gallo said. "Concussion. Medic sent him to a hospital ship, wired his jaw shut for six weeks."

"Ouch."

"Who knows? Maybe I did him a favor. It kept him out of a few recon patrols." Gallo shifted in his seat. "Anyway, this morning I did some research on sports-related deaths. You know what I found?"

Cord shrugged. "What's that?"

"There's been exactly one in Newark's history. This one."

"Seriously?"

"Sure, there's kids jumping into reservoirs, breaking their necks, but I don't consider that a sport. I'm talking about sanctioned sporting events, dating back to the 1800s."

"Well, that's a long time before MMA."

Gallo took out a notepad and glanced at his notes. "MMA. The typical fight goes, what, three rounds?"

"Non-title fights are three rounds, five minutes per round. The title bout in tournaments is five five-minute rounds or until someone taps or gets kayoed."

"And how many fights to get to the finals of one of these tournaments?"

"Depends. Last night it was four wins and you're the champ."

Gallo frowned. "The recovery time for a normal fight is—what, a month?"

Cord nodded. "Maybe longer. The big leagues have mandatory suspensions if you get messed up bad."

"And these tournaments, they make a guy fight *four times* in one night? I'm no expert, but that there doesn't sound safe."

Cord considered Gallo's point. He couldn't disagree: it probably *wasn't* safe. But, hell, he would never complain about fighting too much. It was, after all, the thing he loved most in the world. "The doctor checks you between fights," he responded. "If he thinks you're at risk, he'll DQ you from the tournament and send you to the hospital for observation."

"DQ?" Gallo laughed. "What, you get messed up, and they send you for ice cream?"

Cord had to smile. "DQ means disqualification. If that happens, you'll generally get a sixty- or ninety-day rest before you're cleared to fight again."

"What about during the fight? What protects you, to make sure no one gets beat-up too badly?"

"Getting beat-up is the nature of the sport, Detective, even if you win. Sometimes the winner takes a worse beating than the loser. But the ref is supposed to step in if a guy's getting pummeled and he's unable to defend himself. The tournaments are usually ISCF sanctioned. This one was."

"ISCF?"

"International Sport Combat Federation. They oversee the events. They make sure promoters establish the rules and fighters follow them." Cord wondered if Gallo had already gleaned this information from the promoter. Surely he'd taken his statement, too. Cord decided to play along, for the time being. If Gallo was trying to catch him in a lie—well, that's what cops did, he supposed. But he had nothing to hide, so this all seemed a waste of time.

"Rules like what? No hitting in the groin?"

Cord nodded. "No kicks or knees to the head of a downed opponent, no small joint manipulation—"

Gallo grimaced. "I had a dislocated knuckle in 'Nam. Damn thing never healed right." He held out his hand and made a fist. One knuckle stuck out from the rest like a tumorous growth.

"No doubt," Cord agreed.

"And how did it come about, you two fighting each other?"

"We didn't find out the matchups until ten minutes before the fight."

Gallo jotted something in the pad. He looked up, one eyebrow cocked. "So you didn't plan on fighting?"

"Absolutely not."

"How's it work, the brackets? Is it like the NCAA tourney? Seeds and what not?"

"Nothing that complicated. You'd have to ask the promoter, but I think they probably just throw the names into a hat."

"That sounds pretty random for an ICF-whatever sanctioned event. What's the name of this promoter?"

"Clements, I think."

"You think?"

"I don't remember, exactly. I only spoke to him once on the phone."

"When was this?"

Cord squinted. "Last Tuesday, I think?"

"You don't sound too sure about anything this morning."

Cord felt a bead of sweat on his forehead. He was

afraid to wipe it away, with Columbo eyeing him so closely. "I don't usually log my phone conversations."

"Uh-huh. What's this promoter's first name?"

Cord shrugged. "No idea. He gave me a fax number so my doctor could send a medical release form. That was about the extent of it."

"You ever fight for this promoter before?"

"No."

"What about underground fights, grudge matches? You know, like in the basement of a bar, those kinds of things?"

Cord swallowed hard. Half his fights were unsanctioned events, certainly illegal. "Nope," he said. "Never fought in those."

Gallo eyed him closely. "You sure about that?"

"Those kinds of events aren't exactly good for a guy's career, if you know what I mean. You don't get paid much. You don't get any credit. And you're likely to get hurt."

"I see." The detective checked his notepad. "Tell me more about this event set-up. You say they throw names in a hat?"

"I said I didn't know that for sure," Cord said. "I'm guessing."

"So the winner moves on to the next round? Like the Tough Man competition?"

Cord winced. "Fat man competition, we call it. Most of those guys are drunken slobs. Winner gets extra points for having the biggest beer gut."

"But that's the idea, right? You keep fighting until you lose?"

"Yeah, round robin."

Gallo took a deep breath. "All right. Let's go over this again. I'd like for you to give me a play-by-play of the fight. Let's see if you can recall anything out of the ordinary."

"There's plenty out of the ordinary," Cord said. "My friend died in the cage."

"Besides that."

"Didn't we already go through this last night, Detective?"

"I'd like to hear it again. It's important to understand all the facts, and, trust me, I'm speaking from experience here. At this early juncture in an investigation, you never know what small detail might be important."

"Investigation?"

Gallo waved a hand in the air. "Getting all the facts together so we can close the case."

Cord sighed and took a drink of water. He told Gallo everything he could remember from the fight: the pre-fight introductions, the stare-down, circling each other in the cage—all the way up to the killer right hook. At that point, he paused to collect himself. "And then I saw the opening."

He recalled the way Vic shifted his weight onto his back foot to launch a right of his own, the way he dropped his left hand, leaving his head unprotected.

"Opening?"

"He lowered his guard."

"And you hit him just as hard as you could, a man who had his guard down?"

"Not down. Just a little low."

"Why would a guy lower his guard?"

"I'm not saying he did it on purpose. He made a mistake. That's what we're looking for all the time—one mistake to end the fight."

"Well, you sure ended that sucker."

Cord flinched.

Gallo broke the silence by saying, "So this hook, you practice that a lot?"

"All the time, sure."

"You'd say it's like a trademark of yours?"

"It's my best punch."

"I'm probably dating myself here, but going way back when I was in the academy, they used to teach us a lot about human anatomy. Did you know there are three-hundred some pressure points on the human body?"

"No, I did not."

"You can disable a man just by tapping a nerve in the right spot." Gallo made a jutting motion, stabbing his first two fingers in the air. "You know what else? You can kill a man, if you know where to hit him."

"We study form, not pressure points."

"No, huh?" Gallo studied Cord's face for a moment then snapped shut the notebook. He gave Cord a sheepish smile, his face creasing like old parchment. "My wife says I should show more compassion. But it's part of the job, asking questions. I'm sure you understand." He stuck out a hand.

"No problem, Detective."

"Thanks for your time, Mr. Masland. I'll call if I need anything else."

"I'll be here. Here or the cemetery."

Gallo stopped at the doorway. "Cemetery? What's that, a joke?"

"It's my job. I'm a gravedigger at Woodside, third shift."

"Oh, right." He opened his pad and flipped a page. "I got that right here. How's it pay?"

Cord shrugged. "Lousy. And the hours suck, too."

"Try being a cop."

Gallo left by the kitchen door, limping out to his car.

CHAPTER 3

Cord drove Mercy's car back to his apartment, his friend's rosary beads still dangling from the rearview mirror, his cologne filling Cord's nostrils. He could hardly believe Mercy was gone.

He parked on the curb and went up to ring the doorbell—the moment he'd been dreading all day. At the front door, he noticed a bottle cap on the flagstone and snatched it up. The other night, while sitting on the stoop, he and Mercy had shared a six-pack. It had been the first warm night of the year and one of their favorite things to do—toss back a few and discuss upcoming fights while watching the college girls pass by. *Had been*, he thought. Mercy was now in the past tense, he reminded himself. Twenty-nine years old, zipped in a black body bag. How was that possible? Cord couldn't wrap his brain around the fact. Every time he tried, the neural pathways in his head rebelled.

Kelly answered the door in sweatpants. She was Mercy's live-in girlfriend. They'd dated on and off since high school, though Mercy had never gotten around to popping the question. Marriage, he'd said, wasn't for him. Cord wasn't surprised he'd thought that way with the parental example he'd had.

Mercy's parents had spent most of their waking hours bickering. The fighting tended to peak when his old man came home drunk. It ended when his mother fell down the stairs and broke her neck, a freak accident, when Mercy was ten, leaving him alone with his father for a time.

Kelly's eyes were puffy and red. "Come in, Cord."

"I brought the car," he said stupidly, handing over the keys.

"Put them on the coffee table."

He dropped the keys on top of the new issue of *MMA Sports*—left open to an article about Mercy's favorite fighter, Forrest Griffin. Mercy had admired Forrest because of his tenacity, his unwillingness to quit, even when battered and bloodied. Vic's favorite true story about Forrest: he'd once broken his arm in a fight, only to use the same arm to knock out his opponent later in the round.

"Bourbon," Kelly said, holding a drink. "My third of the day. Want one?"

She looked ten years older: drunk, red-eyed, no makeup. Usually, she wouldn't show herself without a color-coordinated outfit. She spent every third weekend at the Marlene Weber day spa getting body wraps, pedicures, target facials. She would come home reeking of rosemary, sage, and mint, Mercy had told him on more than one occasion. She usually wore her hair back, a sexy school-teacher look that brought out her cheekbones. Now her hair hung into her face, frizzy and unkempt.

"How, Cord? How did this happen?"

He shook his head. "I'm sorry, Kelly—" He paused to wipe away a few tears. He'd always liked her, in a big sister kind of way. Most girlfriends would throw a hissy fit if their man spent as much time with a buddy as he'd spent with Mercy—at least two hours a day in the gym, and that didn't count the long jogs, the beers afterward, the time they spent watching Wreckage and UFC. But not Kelly. She gave Mercy his bro-time, so long as he came home when he said he would and kept it in his pants at the bar. Over the years, Cord grew to appreciate her.

Two years ago, after he broke up with his ex-girlfriend, Liana, Kelly had cooked him dinner every night for a week. Let him talk himself out.

It had helped to have a female's perspective, some-one to raise his spirits. It was Liana's loss, she'd said, not his. Over time, he'd come pretty close to believing her.

She gestured to a picture of Mercy and her standing in front of a divi-divi tree on a beach in Aruba. "It wasn't all sunshine, you know," she said. "He had demons. He tried to kill himself when he was a kid. You knew that, right?"

He nodded. After his parents died, Mercy was shipped to a group home for wayward teens. One day, he slit his wrists over the kitchen sink. A housekeeper found him passed out on the linoleum, blood pooling around his feet. If she hadn't been a former LPN, he probably wouldn't have made it. He was fifteen, covered with ink and piercings, blue-white from loss of blood. After that, he spent three months in a state psych hospital.

"Every time he slipped into depression," she said, "I was there to pick up the pieces. I can't tell you how many times I begged him to stop fighting. He was almost thirty years old. What if we had kids?"

"Vic was terrific with kids. He trained middle-schoolers at the gym on his own time."

"You can't be a father and fight in a cage."

Cord gripped the edge of the couch but said nothing.

"I knew he'd get himself killed one day. I saw it coming."

"What do you mean?"

She stood looking out the window with her hands on her hips. "He threw his life away. And for what, Cord?"

"It's what he loved."

"You two never should've gotten involved in fighting. He'd still be alive today."

"MMA was good for Vic. It helped him with the depression. It gave him a reason to live."

"Are you trying to convince me? Or yourself?"

"I mean before this. It was good for him."

"He was your best friend. Did you really have to hit him that hard?"

He looked away. "I'm sorry."

"Didn't you think someone might get hurt?"

"I never thought this would happen, no."

"How could you not? Two grown men in a ring, punching each other—"

"It's not about fighting—it's about training, discipline. Winning."

"Yeah, well, you wanted to win pretty badly, didn't you?"

"I'm sorry, Kelly. I don't know how many times I can say it—"

Tears fell onto her cheeks, but she made no move to wipe them away. "What am I supposed to do now? Tell me that, Cord."

"I've been asking myself that same question."

"Let me know when you come up with an answer." She staggered toward the kitchen, feeling along the wall for balance. "In the meantime, get the fuck out of my house," she called without turning around.

ೲೣೲ

It was dark by the time Cord got to the cemetery at nine. He parked in front of Rusty's Ford pickup in the glare of the garage floodlights. "Rusty?" he called.

Inside the garage, a single row of fluorescent lights sputtered. The door to the shop, where Rusty kept the tools of the trade—shovels, rakes, pneumatic tampers— was open, allowing a sliver of light to spill out onto the patched concrete. A toilet flushed. A moment later, Rusty emerged from the bathroom, adjusting his coveralls and scratching his bald scalp. "Jesus, Cord. Can't a man take a shit in peace?"

"Sorry."

"You okay?"

"I've been better," Cord admitted.

They both nodded in silence. Cord didn't mind the quiet between them. Living with Lovie and Senator, there was precious little quiet. That was one of the reasons he liked working at Woodside. He only had to answer to Rusty, an old family friend. He'd taught Cord about fishing—where to dig for earthworms, how to bait a hook, when to drag the reel. Some of Cord's best childhood memories were afternoons spent at Mills Pond, relaxing in the sun, listening to the mourning doves. *'You hook a crawler like this, right through the nose.'*

"Mercy's uncle called," said the old man. "Funeral's set for Tuesday, three o'clock. Take off tomorrow night if you want." Rusty took out a tin of Skoal, pinched out a quarter-sized dip, and tucked it into his cheek.

"What's on tap for tonight?"

"Take the floodlights and some Photo-Flo out to D-3. Some idiots knocked your pop's headstone over last night. Damned if I know why they'd want to do a thing like that or how they did it. I righted it with the tank this afternoon."

"What else did they do?"

Halloween, two years before, someone had scribbled swear words on headstones and some of the mausoleums. Cord had worked for hours scrubbing off a spray-painted penis on a stone carving of the Station of the Cross. Another time, a teenager had halfway exhumed a corpse before Rusty chased him away, leaving Cord to refill the grave. At night, the problem wasn't the dead getting out, it was the living getting in.

"Nothing. Just your pop's grave."

"You call the cops?"

Rusty spat. "You know what I think about cops."

"What else?"

"That's it."

"Look, Rusty, I can dig Vic's grave—"

"I'll handle that one."

Cord opened his mouth to protest, but Rusty held up a hand, ending the discussion. "Make sure the gate's locked. And water the magnolias, they're startin' to bloom."

After Rusty left, Cord glanced up the hill. On the crest was Holy Reckoning Church, where Father Reginald would perform Tuesday's service, and to the right, Moog's Funeral Home, overlooking the highway. Would Mercy's body be there right now? Cord hoped it wasn't. Dead bodies were the nature of his business—but the thought of Mercy lying on a cold steel slab made his stomach keel.

Funeral Tuesday. That was fine. But he wouldn't go to the wake. He didn't need to see Mercy in his coffin— mannequin face waxy smooth, eyes glued shut, skin covered with enough makeup for a sorority house.

Cord straightened up the shop. He sprinkled sand on the grease and gasoline streaks on the concrete where Rusty had been working on the power mowers. Around midnight, he walked the perimeter of the graveyard with a flashlight. He wished he'd worn a heavier jacket. The air had dropped the pretense of spring like a pole dancer shedding her birth name. The trees outside the fence swayed drunkenly in the breeze. His flashlight settled on a pair of yellow eyes high up in the branches: an owl, curled around itself in the night air.

At the shop, he picked up a floodlight, a bucket of warm water, and a bottle of Photo-Flo, a non-ionic detergent that didn't tear up the headstones as it cleaned them. He went out to D-3, as Rusty called it. Cord thought of the sections in more poetic terms—Willow's Corner, Brookside, East Lawn. East Lawn was where his parents' graves were located. He'd been avoiding that part of the cemetery since his father Stanley died the year before. Stan's headstone made him nervous. The old man hadn't approved of Cord—not in his martial arts training, his choice of friends, or his job. Cord wasn't worth much, according to Stanley. After hearing that diatribe for the good part of twenty-nine years, and given what had happened last night, Cord found it hard to argue.

He followed a grassy path between lines of head-stones, stopping at the graves. Stanley's headstone read *Sheet Metal Worker, Local 28, NY*. It was made of flecked marble, a foot taller than Barbara's, which read simply, *Loving Mother*. That she had been, except for later in life, when anxiety sank its teeth in and bit down hard, and she'd chosen survival in the form of little blue pills.

A clump of sod clung to the facing of his father's stone with grass streaks staining the surface. Why would someone trash his dad's headstone? His father hadn't made many friends in life, true, but he also hadn't had many enemies. Stan had made a slew of *acquaintances*: bar buddies, neighbors, coworkers. He had been a sheet metal worker for forty-five years. He'd once dragged Cord to a trade show in Amenia. Stan had probably intended to spark interest in the boy—ten at the time—but all it gave him were a series of dim nightmares remembering the gap-toothed drills and shears, saws, and presses that buzzed to life with deafening shrieks.

A mere handful of Stan's acquaintances showed up at his funeral to hear Father Reginald's eulogy, barely enough to fill the first two pews. His family didn't even show. According to Stan, his brother Frank was a good-for-nothing moneygrubber. His sister was too chatty, his brother-in-law a liar. He even had a problem with his younger brother Jordan, who'd lost both legs in Vietnam. Jordan, said Stan, was a leech, working the system on his disability. "Boy, you have to take initiative in life," he liked to say to Cord at the dinner table. "Grow up, stop raising hell at school. A trade would be the best thing. A little sheet metal work ought to take the fight out of you."

No wonder so few people came to his funeral, Cord thought. Who wanted to memorialize a man who hadn't had a kind word for anyone? And who the hell would take the effort to knock down his headstone?

Cord knelt and pulled the squeegee out of the bucket. The suds dribbled over his arms. He dabbed at the stone, washing away the grime and grass stains. A few of the smudges wouldn't come out, and pretty soon he found himself scrubbing the marble with a sawing motion that brought jewels of sweat to his forehead.

When he moved around to the other side of the stone, he noticed a photograph on the ground. Cord smoothed it out on his leg, and his eyes widened in surprise. It was a picture of Mercy and him battling each other in the cage. Mercy wore his red KDDO trunks—the same trunks he wore the prior night. The two of them were throwing simultaneous punches, each connecting, Mercy a straight right, Cord a hook to the temple—*the punch*. Cord looked up, dumbfounded. Someone had been at the fight, snapped this picture, then came out and left it here. But why?

He turned the photo over. He squinted to read the inscription in the glare from the floodlights, sounding out the words aloud: "*Per is vomica ego excito abyssus subvertio meus animus.*"

He heard a sound and glanced to the edge of the woods. A figure loomed in the glare of the floodlights on the other side of the fence. Cord caught his breath. It was a huge man, a giant almost as tall as the eight-foot iron posts. He held a shovel in his hand.

Cord recoiled, landing on his ass. "Hey!" he called, his voice reed-thin in the cold air. "We're closed. You can't be here."

The man tossed the shovel over the fence, grabbed the top rail, and hauled himself up. Cord got to his feet, undecided whether to run back to the shop or stay and watch what would happen next.

Were his eyes playing tricks? He'd never seen a bigger man—not even the Norseman who'd cracked his arm in two at that Atlantic City Bar. "I'm warning you, buddy."

The man looped a leg over the top rail, straddled the fence for a moment, then dropped to the other side. Cord stuffed the photo in his pocket. He clenched his fists and felt the periphery of his vision narrowing to a singular focus, his pre-fight concentration.

The giant advanced with a light-footed quickness, surprising for such a big man. He grinned as he approached, brandishing the shovel. As Cord set himself to deliver a rising front-kick to the balls—illegal in MMA but perfectly acceptable for graveyard night-fighting—he noticed the man's eyes, one of them glossy white in the muted lighting, the other pure black.

Can't be, Cord thought.

Then the big man was on him faster than seemed possible, swinging the shovel in a wide arc. It whistled toward Cord's head before he could move. He raised his arm to block it, deflecting some of the blow, but the shovel struck Cord's temple with a crack he heard *inside* his head, and there was the sense of weightless falling.

THREE DAYS...

CHAPTER 4

Cord woke to a splash of cold water on his face. Rusty stared down at him, holding the empty bucket. The early morning daylight blitzed his vision, and Cord held up a hand to shield his eyes. "What the hell?"

"That's what I'd like to know."

Cord pushed himself up on his elbows, grimacing. A huge purple welt had formed on his forearm, spurring his memory from the night before. The big man, the shovel. Cord would be lucky if the arm wasn't broken. He glanced around, but the movement made him dizzy. "Where is he?"

"Who?"

"The guy—"

Rusty pointed toward Cord's parents' gravesite. "That's more work than you've done for the past month. But *why* you done it is a mystery to me."

Cord looked at the freshly dug grave—six feet deep—next to his father's.

An unfinished headstone was wedged into the dirt at the head of the grave.

Dean Masland
Born
September 7, 1986
Died
April 15, 2016
In fronte praecipitium, a tergo lupi.
Abyssus expectat.

Underneath was a symbol:

死

"That supposed to be some kind of joke?" Rusty asked.

Cord shook his head. He'd been around enough Chinese martial artists to know what *that* sign meant.

Death.

⌘⌘⌘

Back home, Cord pulled the photograph from his pants pocket. He stared at it, wondering if his eyes were playing tricks. The photo was blank, like photographic film that'd been prematurely exposed to light. *What the hell?* He turned it over, searching for the words that had been written there. "I've got to be losing my mind."

He took his laptop downstairs to the kitchen. A quick internet search on the message carved into the headstone confirmed his suspicions of Latin origin. It read, *The precipice in front, the wolf behind. The abyss awaits.*

A decidedly lovely message. "Wonderful," he said aloud.

"What is?" Lovie said, entering the kitchen and removing a carton of milk from the fridge.

"Forget it."

"What's that ink on your neck say? You get that done at Ace's?"

"I don't want to talk about it."

"So you got some drunk ink. Big deal." Lovie pulled up his shirt, exposing rolls of doughy flesh, a cavernous navel, and a tattoo of his ex-girlfriend, Mindy Shepherd, running the length of his upper torso. "Last week I got blitzed and tatted-up—and we broke up *nine years ago.* But you don't see me crying about it."

"And you think that's normal?"

"You're never going to guess who I ran into today."

"Who?"

"You probably don't want to know."

"Then why'd you bring it up?"

Lovie shrugged. "Liana. I saw her coming out of the diner. She asked about you."

"What'd you tell her?"

"I told her you're good."

"What else?"

"I told her you've been banging a stripper—you

know, so she knows you've moved on."

Cord forced himself to relax. *Lovie means well*, he thought, *he really does*.

"She looked pretty damn hot, bro. You don't mind me saying that, do you?" Lovie made a move to leave then poked his head around the corner. "Oh, and I told her about Mercy. She didn't know."

Liana. The name made Cord's insides clutch. He'd met her his senior year at Pace, and they'd dated for six years. She'd been an actress, quirky, dynamic, full of life. At the end, she'd locked herself in her apartment for days, read Nietzsche, and refused to answer his calls.

Cord didn't hate her, not really. He'd sealed away all the memories: watching her onstage—Ophelia, Juliet, Lysistrata—the long afternoons at Sterling Lake, the sex in the back of his Celica, her fingernails digging softly into the back of his neck. "'A pair of powerful spectacles has sometimes sufficed to cure a person in love,'" he said, quoting Nietzsche, his voice echoing in the kitchen silence. It was one of her influences, one of the few he hadn't been able to cleanse from his system. She taught him a lot of philosophy and theater during their time together, dropping names and one-liners. He supposed it was his way of hanging onto a piece of her after she was gone, even if it was only a splinter under his skin.

"You look like you need a hug." The voice had an odd click to it, a rattling lisp. Senator had his tongue ring in. "What'd you do to your head this time?"

Cord considered trying to explain the previous night but saw no point. If it didn't make sense to him, it wouldn't to anyone else. Had he dreamed the whole thing? He could've convinced himself he did—if not for the bruises. "Hit my head at work."

Senator had just stepped out of the shower. He was thin, his skin milky-white. He had a ring through his right nipple. Cord wondered how Senator's father, Brady Valor, a conservative Connecticut congressman who'd fought a losing battle to ban gay marriage in the state, felt about body art.

Senator frowned. "You did that to yourself, didn't you?"

"I just told you how I did it."

"You need help, dude. You've suffered a trauma. You should see a professional. I'll make you an appointment with my spiritual advisor." Senator was into tarot cards, numerology, palm readings. If a woman had the word *Madame* in her name, Senator took her seriously. He went to Inamorata a couple of times a week, a hole-in-the-wall on Fox Street, home to High Falls's most notable psychic, Madame Celeste.

"I'm fine, Senator, really."

"You're not, man. Take a look in the mirror. Besides your physical injuries, your energy is all fucked up. Rest won't fix that." He pulled a business card from his wallet and tucked it into Cord's front pocket. "In case you change your mind."

Cord didn't believe in ghosts. He dismissed Senator's psychic as the most harmless of charlatans. At least psychics, in essence, told people what they wanted to hear. But how could he explain what had happened to him the past two days? Mystery tattoos, pictures that appeared and disappeared, freshly dug graves with his name on them. The bearded freak in the lab coat, appearing first in his dream, then in the graveyard. All paranoid delusions? The knot on his forehead suggested otherwise.

Someone was out to kill him. He understood that much. He could *feel* it, the sensation of being pursued. He wanted to tell someone, but what could he say that wouldn't get him locked up in Hudson Psych? He pictured walking into a police station, mumbling about tattoos and giants that appeared out of nowhere. Who would take him seriously?

"'There was the door to which I found no key; there was the veil through which I might not see,'" he whispered to himself.

It was useless, pondering the unexplainable. He needed to get the blood flowing, to do the one thing that always calmed his anxiety: get to the gym.

CHAPTER 5

Pound-for-Pound was the grimiest gym in the Hudson Valley. Once, Cord saw a rat the size of Leonidas plodding across the downstairs weight room. Not the place for made-up girls in halter tops or lunk alarms. At Pound-for-Pound, dudes didn't feel at home unless they were juicing. Cord himself shot up once, a cycle of Deca-Durabolin some years back, before some of the promoters started testing. But it wasn't his thing—the bipolar emotions, the massive bloating, and cramping, like PMS tinged with uncontrollable rage, he'd imagined. But at Pound-for-Pound, guys looked the other way when you roid-raged, slammed the weights, punched a hole in the wall. In the free-weight rooms, the primal grunting echoed off the walls like the mating calls of lions. Metal music roared from overhead speakers. Crack vials littered the front entrance. An ideal place to train.

Outside, it was a mild sixty-five; inside, it was incinerator room hot. Wall fans did little but push around the hot air, tinged with sweat and a wild-boar odor. Shrieking guitars ripped through the speakers, jacking his pulse into the one hundred plus range—well, that and the Red Bull he'd inhaled on the drive over. In the corner, a couple of no-necks strained for the extra rep that would either put them over the top or send them to the hospital. He nodded a greeting to Mad Dog, the muscle head behind the front desk, but kept his mouth shut. At Pound-for-Pound, the only things dudes got to know well were their own physical limits.

Cord slipped on his open-palm MMA gloves and started on the heavy bag. The bag lurched with each hit, the ceiling joists creaking under its weight. Before long, he was oozing sweat. Jab, jab, uppercut, hook. The blows eased his anxiety—Mercy's death, the cataract-gaze of...the Coroner...he didn't know what else to call the man he'd seen twice now, once in a dream and once in the physical realm.

Finally, he rolled off his gloves and went to the rear window. Beneath him, Hamburg Creek gurgled past, all mottled brown water and moldering leaves. A light breeze cooled the sweat on his forehead. On the calendar, spring was already a few weeks past, but this felt like the first *real* day of spring. Along the creek's bank, green buds sprouted nascent leaves. A squirrel ran along a bare limb, bounding from tree to tree.

"Hey, Cord," a voice called from behind. "You want to roll?"

Cord turned. Vinnie Lombardo, an ex-juicehead

turned Brazilian Jiu-Jitsu practitioner. He'd been Cord's on-and-off training partner for the past few years. Vinnie stood at five foot seven, two inches shorter than Cord, with a nose like the beak of a hawk. His long black hair was tied back in a ponytail. Cord never understood why some MMA guys wore long hair. Pulling hair might be frowned upon in the UFC, but it was *encouraged* in the no-holds-barred events Cord participated in.

"As long as you don't mind the sweat. I just got done hitting the bag."

Vinnie grinned and bro-hugged him. "Just don't right-hook me, okay, man?"

Cord sighed. Vinnie meant well, he figured. He was just too stupid to know when not to make a joke. "No, man."

"I'm just trying to make you laugh. A tragedy."

"Thanks, bro."

They ran through a few stretches then practiced grappling from the clinch, using Judo leg throws and single-leg takedowns to haul each other to the mat. Once, Cord landed on top in full mount position. Vinnie rolled over on his stomach—giving up his back—and Cord pushed his weight down, flattening out his training partner and securing a full-body triangle with his right leg tight across Vinnie's midsection.

Cord could hear Vinnie wheezing for breath; the triangle was like having an anaconda wrapped around your body, crushing your ribcage, squeezing off your airways. Finally, he locked his forearm across Vinnie's throat and grabbed his bicep, using the other hand to push Vinnie's head forward into the hold until he tapped. Rear naked choke.

"Not bad," Vinnie said, sitting up and massaging his throat. "The batwings were closing in."

Cord nodded. "Been there before." Getting choked out felt like the wings of some enormous bird eclipsing your field of vision. When the blackness was complete…well, that meant nap time.

"You ever get choked out in a fight?"

"Close. I tapped before I blacked out," Cord admitted. "Better than risking cerebral infarction."

Vinnie grinned. "A what?"

"A stroke, dumbass."

Cord used a towel to wipe the sweat from his forehead, balled it up, and lobbed it into the corner. "You?"

"I never stroked out. But I shattered a foot on some dude's skull, that time in New Rochelle."

"Give me a break, Vin. You tripped getting into the cage."

Vinnie winked. "That's not what I tell the ladies."

The locker room smelled of piss and ammonia. A codger walked out of the shower stall holding a towel. He wore paper flip flops and nothing else. Cord quickly averted his eyes and hurried past. *What was it with old guys*, Cord wondered, *always displaying their wrinkled junk? You got a towel; put it on.*

Mad Dog leaned over a urinal, one arm propped against the tiled wall. He wore a yellow bandanna, an XXXL T-shirt, and tiger-striped Zubaz pants. He studied Cord as he entered. "Yo, Masland."

Cord nodded at him.

"You're a wanted man around here."

"How's that?"

Mad Dog piss-shivered, zipped, and turned toward Cord with a grin. "Cop came around this morning looking for you."

"Old dude, trench coat?"

"That's him."

"What'd he want?"

"You. He asked if you ever had issues with any of the people here. He wanted to know if you had a temper." Mad Dog ran water over his hands then cranked the paper towel dispenser like he was hauling in a fifty-pound catfish. Finding it empty, he reared back and punched it, denting the metal siding with the sound of a gunshot report. He dried his hands on his pants and said over his shoulder, "I told him you and I like to cuddle during Lifetime movies."

"Thanks a lot, Mad Dog. I knew I could always count on you."

Mad Dog put a meat hook on Cord's shoulder. Cord had the idea that all it would take was one twist and his shoulder would separate like pulled pork. "Don't worry, killer. I didn't say a word. Nobody did."

Cord nodded. When he tugged off his shirt to shower a few minutes later, a business card fell to the floor. He examined it.

Madame Celeste, LLC
Certified Astral Psychic and Medium

She travels beyond the Nebulous Veil.
Dare to travel with her?
Walk-ins welcome!
Inamorata / 1331 Fox Street
High Falls, New York 12666
(555) 555-5431
spiritlovr1@itt.com

"Why not?" he said aloud. Given the past couple of days, he figured a psychic consultation couldn't do him any harm.

ᘒᕟᘒᕟ

Inamorata was wedged between a billiards hall and a dog kennel. The ethereal sounds of Enya filtered from a pair of speakers, warring with the manic yapping of the kenneled dogs. He glanced above the awning at the lavender and pink sign pockmarked with spiral galaxy drawings: *Inamorata cares about the spiritual health of its customers.* A heavyset blonde woman with long false eyelashes and cat's-eye glasses emerged from the entrance, raising her doughy arms skyward, the loose skin quivering.

"Isn't it wonderful?" she asked.

Cord looked behind him, but he was the only person in the vicinity. "I'm sorry?"

The woman gave him a push meant to be playful but felt more like a Heisman stiff-arm. "The feeling you get when you step out."

He shrugged. "It's my first time."

The woman squealed with delight. "You're so lucky." She reached to touch his face. "My late husband gave me my first appointment as a Christmas gift, the only good thing he ever did for me." Her eyes filmed over with tears as she continued to her car.

Senator met him at the front door. Inside, it smelled like cinnamon, sugar cookies, cucumbers, melons—incense candles. Red curtains hung from the walls, as if the owners were about to unveil artwork. Neon pinwheels dangled from the ceiling, revolving lazily in the breeze from the fan.

"I just finished my interlude," Senator said. He breathed in deep, eyes closed, holding out his arms like he'd been nailed to an invisible cross.

"Interlude?" Cord wondered if they had a fancy term for taking a crap: *the hallowed purge*.

The curtains rustled, and Kelly, Vic's girlfriend, stepped out from the backroom. She split time between working front desk and sales at Inamorata and running her own home decorating service. To Cord, she looked better than the day before: high heels, a multi-colored skirt, white chemise with a bodice pulled tight to her torso, breasts heaving out the top.

When she saw him, her eyes widened. "What the fuck are you doing here—"

"I invited him," Senator broke in.

"You made an appointment?"

"No."

Kelly ran a finger down the logbook. "I'm sorry. I

don't have anything until next Thursday."

Senator grabbed Cord's arm. "It's an emergency."

"Wait!" Kelly said.

Senator led him through the curtains. For a few moments, Cord was lost in the folds, smothered in red velvet. Finally, he spilled into a circular room with a platform in the center, sloping up like a pitcher's mound. At the apex, two low Asian chairs flanked a table with a rounded object atop covered by a thin tablecloth—a crystal ball, he imagined, although he'd never seen one before. A doorway was cut out of the side wall with beaded rope hanging across the opening.

"Madame Celeste?" Senator called out. "Are you here?"

"Come back here," yelled Kelly.

The beads parted, and Madame Celeste appeared. She wore a flowing white robe that dragged behind her like a chapel train and white arm-length gloves. Her hair was flaming red.

"Yes, John?" Celeste said.

Cord realized he'd never heard anyone address Senator by his birth name.

"It's for my friend, Madame. It's an emergency."

Celeste sailed forward, saying, "Mr…"

"Masland," Cord volunteered.

"Mr. Masland is in luck. I am available for one session."

"How much—"

Senator winked. "It's on me, bro."

Cord shuddered at the thought of how much these

"sessions" must cost. Senator, however, had no money concerns. He was set for life in that department, as long as his parents didn't disown him.

"Then have a seat, Mr. Masland."

"Call me Corduroy."

"Corduroy?" She pulled a hood over her head and motioned to the raised platform at the center. When he didn't move, Senator nudged him in the back.

Cord took a seat, realizing it was way too short—his head barely crested the table's edge. He turned to say something, but Celeste was already settling into her chair, folding her legs underneath Indian-style. With the white robe spilling onto the floor, she looked like a candle dripping wax. Her posture was ironing-board straight. When he tried to imitate her pose, his knees barked from the strain, so he settled on a kneeling half-crouch. Senator stood to the side with his hands clasped together. Celeste extended her hands palms-up on the white tablecloth and closed her eyes. Cord took her hands. They were surprisingly warm—hot, almost.

"You have much stress within," she said. "It acts like poison."

"You don't know the half of it."

She frowned. "Close your eyes, please, and be quiet."

He felt the pull of her voice, like a rip current tugging him from shore. After a few moments, he became conscious of suctioning on his fingertips. Something was flowing out through his fingers. He could *feel* it. He had the urge to open his eyes, see how she was doing it—

"Please do not open your eyes."

Strange, but he began to feel better. The anxiety of the past few days slowly leached from his system.

She's hypnotizing me, he thought.

"Now turn out the light, Corduroy."

When she said his name, he felt an electric tingle up his spine. He felt weightless. A spiral galaxy materialized out of the blackness with phosphorescent light swirling toward a golden center.

"You are weightless now."

She was waiting for something. Something he was supposed to say. Without thinking, he opened his mouth and words tumbled out. "What do you know of me?"

The siphoning feeling in his fingertips increased. "Dean Masland. Your mother and your father are both in the astral plane. You have a brother." She paused, made a clicking sound in her throat. "A half-brother."

When he spoke, he couldn't keep out the sadness in his voice. "What happened to Mercy?"

"He, too, is in the astral plane, by the hand of God."

Cord felt tears on his cheeks.

"I am also sensing deep pain and unrequited love. A woman. Your destinies travel in opposite directions. Something is forcing you apart."

"What's happening to me?"

"Come back to me, now." The impression of floating ceased. He returned to his body but had no desire to open his eyes. Celeste smiled—he could feel her smile. "Let's go a little deeper."

The pull on his fingers heightened.

"Something has changed. *You* have changed. I'm sensing a different aura—"

The tattoo on the back of his neck flared, a brilliant bolt of pain. "What is it?"

"Death."

Senator gasped.

"There is an evil force—" Her hands trembled under his. "—a tall bearded man."

"The Coroner. What does he want?"

"He wants what all demons want."

Instinctively, he understood. What did demons want if not human souls? "Tell me what to do."

"He is reaching out, attempting to make contact." Suddenly, her arms were spasming, threatening to buck off his hands. "The source," she cried out.

When she pulled her hands away, Cord opened his eyes. Celeste was gone. The Coroner sat across the table from him. His cataract eye winked grotesquely. The other eye stared in complete blackness.

Cord reeled back, but the Coroner's hand shot out, hooking his arm. Then the scenery at Inamorata faded, and they were standing on a blood-spattered canvas mat in an octagon cage. Through the fencing, Cord could see the eyes of spectators all around the perimeter—not their faces, only their white eyes in the darkness. He sensed uniformity among the spectators. The idea occurred to him that they might be parts of one conglomerate: CROWD. They began to jeer and whistle catcalls. Cord tried to wrench his arm free, but the Coroner held him tight.

The audience was waiting for something to happen, and the Coroner readied himself to oblige. Reaching down, he took the inlaid tablecloth—still covering what Cord thought of as a crystal ball—and snatched it away.

Underneath was Mercy's decapitated head.

Cord couldn't look away. One eye was blackened. The temple dripped stringy-red tendons and flayed skin as if a bomb had gone off inside his head. *I did that*, Cord thought. *That one's on me.*

The Coroner kicked the head, sending it tumbling across the canvas, and the CROWD went wild—clapping without hands, screaming without mouths. The Coroner reached for Cord's neck, but he scrambled back, parrying the hands out of the way. He jutted a shovel-punch to the Coroner's throat, which would've staggered a normal man. Instead, the Coroner grinned, with teeth like fencepost spikes. Cord threw a desperate right hook—the same punch that'd ended Mercy's life—but the Coroner deftly side-stepped and simultaneously drove a fist into Cord's gut.

He'd been hit by body punches before, by professionals twice his size—but never a blow like this one. He felt it deep in his internal organs, like concussive blasts. The Coroner threw his arms back and pounded his chest, allowing Cord to stagger back to the fence. An electric shock ran through his body as his skin touched the metal. The Coroner was on top of him in an instant, landing a right cross on his chin with a crunch that made his teeth click together. Pain exploded through his jaw, and he fell forward, slamming his head on the canvas. A light show danced in his vision—but years of training had conditioned him to hang onto his consciousness.

Cord crawled to his knees. The Coroner reared back and kicked Cord's injured ribs. Then a fist to the back of his neck. Cord felt himself fading. His tattoo pulsed weakly. The Coroner stood over him, his face convulsed in rage. He reached down and clutched Cord's neck. Then an arc of white light lanced the Coroner's body. The canvas underneath wavered. White hands emerged from a gaping hole in the Coroner's chest. Celeste's form followed, slicing through the demon's body.

When she touched him, the cage disappeared.

Cord found himself lying on soft carpeting, Celeste's hands slipping underneath his body, propping his head up in her lap. Instead of the sweat-reeked stink of canvas, he smelled patchouli.

CHAPTER 6

Celeste crouched over him, telling him to relax.
"Where did he go?" It hurt to talk. His tongue felt swollen and numb. He tried to sit up, but she pushed him gently back.

"Stay still." She wiped at her nose, and her hand came away bloody.

He looked wildly around the room. He'd felt like this only once before, a year earlier, when he'd gotten knocked out by a short Mexican fighter. His trainer, Logan Gears, told him he'd taken a hook kick to the temple and had spent thirty seconds on the canvas, legs twitching, eyes rolled back. He didn't see the kick, didn't remember a thing except walking into the cage.

When the room stopped spinning, he struggled to his elbows. Celeste dropped into a chair, throwing a hand across her brow. His foot nudged a hard object—black marble surface, oddly translucent—the crystal ball.

"Where's Senator?"

Celeste's red hair clung to her damp forehead. "Who?"

"John."

"He fainted." Celeste struggled to her feet. "I'm sorry, but I must ask you to leave."

"Wait. You have to help me. How can I stop him?"

"Please. You must go."

Senator appeared between the velvet curtains. He wiped a hand across his mouth and grimaced. "Does anyone have a breath mint?"

❧❧❧

Cord pulled into his driveway behind a Buick Regal with a dented fender and black tinted windows. He got out of the car, scratching the back of his neck, a surge of irritability running through him like a current.

He peered into the Buick's windows but could only make out his own reflection. A moment later the car door opened, startling him.

"Mr. Masland," Gallo said, tipping his hat.

"D—Detective," Cord stuttered.

"You seem a little jumpy."

"You surprised me."

Gallo climbed out and slammed the car door. "Since our talk yesterday, a few more questions have occurred to me."

Why am I not surprised? Cord thought. "Come on in. Senator should be back. I could have him put on a fresh pot of coffee."

"I'm not that brave. What does he put in that stuff?"

"Secret recipe, he says."

"Ex-Lax, I'd guess." Gallo's smile faded. He took out his notepad, opened it, and frowned. "I spoke to a Mr. Clements this morning. The event promoter. He told me something interesting."

"What's that?"

"He said someone—he's not sure who—called a week ahead to set up your match with Mr. Mercy."

"That's impossible."

"He seemed pretty sure of it."

"Well, it wasn't me, if that's what you're getting at." Cord shielded his eyes from the late sun. "And I can't imagine it was Vic, either."

"No?" Gallo scribbled in the notebook.

"On the drive over, he said to me, 'Maybe we'll see each other in the finals.' Neither of us wanted to face each other before that."

"And why's that?"

"Because, if we met before then, it'd mean one of us was going home early. And like I told you, he was my best friend. We were always rooting for each other."

Gallo nodded. "Except when you're fighting each other, right? You're not rooting for each other then, or else one of you would've taken a dive."

"I suppose. I never thought about it that way."

"That brings me to my next question. You say he's your best friend, but I hear you had it out for this guy."

"Had it out?"

"Had a beef with him. Is there any truth to that?"

"None whatsoever."

"I've been told by more than one individual that he stole your girlfriend. That he slept with her. Is that correct?"

"Who told you that?"

Gallo looked up, one eyebrow raised. "I'm asking the questions, son."

Cord sighed. "I knew Vic since the second grade."

"That doesn't answer my question."

Cord grunted. "The answer is yes. Technically. But I didn't hold any grudge. It was between her and me."

"*Her* would be Liana Sénécal, yes?" Gallo pronounced her last name *Cynical*.

"SEH-neh-kal," Cord said. "She's French Canadian."

"Tell me about her."

"Is that necessary, Detective? I mean, she's got nothing to do with this."

"I'd say she's relevant, given the circumstances."

"Relevant to what?"

"Motive."

"Look, Detective," Cord said. "I've been up front with you. I've told you everything I know—"

"Not exactly everything. You left out the girl, for example."

Cord rubbed his eyes. "We dated in college. I met her at a frat party. She was wearing bellbottoms and a shirt that said *Drama Geek*. We were together six years—until she and Vic got drunk one night and fell into bed. Did I hold it against him? Sure, for about a week. Until we had a six-pack and talked it out. Do I still see her? No, not once in the past two years."

"Have you talked to her?"

"Haven't seen her *or* talked to her."

"Now, you say you and he talked it out. I find that difficult to believe. He sleeps with your girlfriend and you talk, hug, and get on with dinner?"

"Yeah."

"No. That doesn't wash, Mr. Masland. Someone sleeps with my girlfriend of six years, I don't talk or hug. I beat the daylights out of him. I maybe even hold a grudge. A homicidal one."

"Well, that's you, Detective. Not me."

"I got to say it's a little strange, coming from a guy who makes a living with his fists." Gallo closed his notebook. "I'm still trying to get a hold of Mr. Mercy's doctor. The man's vacationing in the Bahamas."

Cord watched Gallo climb back into his car and back out.

☙❧☙❧

Inside, Cord confronted Lovie in the kitchen. "You," Cord said, stiff-arming him against the wall. "What did you tell him?"

Lovie held up his hands. "Take it easy, Cord. He was parked out there for an hour. All I told him was the truth: Mercy stole Liana from you. That prick."

"Why would you tell him something like that?"

Lovie tried on a grin. "I thought it'd earn you some sympathy points."

"That's a motive for murder, you dumb fuck."

"Sorry, dude. I didn't think of that."

Cord shouldered past Lovie. He banged through his bedroom door and rested on the bed, trying to calm down. He noticed his answering machine, blinking. A call from Liana, ten minutes before. Two years without a word, now this. He hit the button.

"Cord, I'm so sorry. I have to tell you something about Vic. Call me. It's important…"

He replayed the message. The pauses, the silence, the inflections. There was fear in her voice, not sympathy. She was scared, and she wanted help. He'd vowed, long ago, never to talk to her again. But now—now that Mercy was gone, now that the Coroner had appeared—none of that seemed to matter. He remembered, all at once, everything he'd been shutting out. The afternoons at Sterling Lake, the way she whispered to him in French during sex, the promise they'd made, their secret.

He noticed something unusual in the fish tank: one of his bloodfin tetras was belly-up at the surface, missing a huge chunk of its crimson tail. "Jesus, Lulu. Did you do that?" She was a velvety shade of dark purple with sweeping fins eclipsing her torso, demon-red eyes with a stripe of amethyst. She stared at him with her fins undulating, the long whiskers on her chin twitching. "What's gotten into you?"

He sprinkled food into the tank and watched as the flakes dispersed toward the bottom. One chunk floated by Lulu's mouth, but she made no attempt to snatch at it. "I get it, you're missing Rocky. So am I, but we have to keep our heads above water. Well, not in your case."

He felt something tugging at him—something he needed to hold in his hands. He rifled through his closet, finding Bruce Lee's fighting stick hidden beneath layers of clothes, out of sight from his housemates. His most prized possession, a gift from his uncle Jordan, the same uncle who'd lost both legs in Nam, falling into a Punji stake trap. Before that, he'd been a boxer and martial arts aficionado, crazy for Yip Man, Dan Inosanto, and, of course, Bruce Lee. After the war, he attended conventions and seminars and met Paul Vunak, who had collected some of Bruce Lee's gear. Vunak awarded Jordan the fighting stick at the end of the three-day seminar, saying he'd pushed himself harder and had complained less than anyone else. In turn, a few months after he was diagnosed with stomach cancer, Jordan gave the stick to Cord. He was buried in the Brookside section of the cemetery, far from the East Lawn and Stanley's plot, a grave Cord visited more often than his dad's.

Under the same pile of clothes, he found a single *Title* fighting glove. Mercy's glove. Tucked into the glove, he found what he wanted: a bloodstained piece of paper, neatly folded into thirds. The paper was coming apart, frazzled at the edges and oily from worrying fingers. It was a poem he'd written for Liana, the ink faded but still legible. He had pieced together the paper from the sayings of her favorite philosophers:

> *They say, at the touch of love, we free*
> *a poet, but there is always some lunacy*

> *in love, not constrained by mastery, when*
> *the hottest love has the coldest end...*

He frowned. An awful poem. He'd written it for her after they'd broken up, during the long nights at the cemetery, when the only thing around for comfort was the wailing of the owls in the trees. He'd recited it aloud, pacing the rows of headstones, his breath chilling out between his lips. Like most acts of masochism, it dulled the pain.

After finishing the poem, he'd picked up a dozen red roses, feeling as giddy as a man about to propose. He wouldn't go that far—but he did have the ring. Liana had wanted to wait. Even after six years, the thought of living together freaked her out. At that time, she'd been acting in commercials for local businesses, her prospects for fame dwindling as she inched toward her thirtieth birthday. Cord, a nighttime gravedigger, then as now, bought the ring with the meager sum he'd inherited from his father. He'd been waiting for the right moment. But then she'd slipped into a depression and started treating him like an extra in one of her plays. The ring made its way to the bottom of his dresser, where it had stayed.

He'd thought the poem and roses might change her mind. He'd knocked at her door. Her mother answered. Josée Sénécal, from Quebec, had worked most of her life as a nurse. She'd married twice, the first time to a French Canadian, Liana's birth father, who'd skipped town when she was an infant. The second husband was a high school gym teacher from Binghamton who boozed until he passed out every night. He'd left too, a few years earlier.

In bare feet, Josée stood an inch above Cord; in heels, she was a skyscraper. She'd passed her good looks down to her daughter—auburn hair, high cheekbones, hazel eyes, neat figure. Standing in the doorway, she narrowed her eyes at Cord. She considered him a deadbeat, not good enough to breathe the same air as her daughter. He didn't have any of the things Liana needed in a man: money, class, a respectable job. He was pretty certain the best day of her life was when Liana and he had broken up.

"She's not home, Dean."

He peered around the half-open door. "I have something for her." He held the roses in one hand, the poem in the other.

"I can see that. But that doesn't change the facts. I'll take it, if you like." She cracked the door another foot and reached for the vase.

"I'd like to give them to her myself."

"I just told you—"

"Her Civic's in the driveway, Mrs. Sénécal."

Josée sighed. "Dean, try to understand this. She doesn't want anything to do with you."

"I don't believe you."

"If you have any decency, you'll leave her alone." Josée made a move to close the door, and Cord—instinctively, stupidly—stuck his foot in the doorjamb. To his amazement, Josée stabbed down on his sneaker with her high heel. He yelped in pain and lurched forward, the door bumping open, the vase sliding out of his hands and smashing on the tile. Josée squawked like a startled swan. Glass skittered across the floor.

"You can't come barging into my house like this," she shouted. "I should call—"

Then, from the top of the stairs: "*Dean?*"

Dean.

Liana never called him Dean. She stood in a robe, her hair still wet from the shower. She looked pale, almost sickly. He realized he was cut, his hand filling with blood.

"You can't be here."

"I need to talk to you. Five minutes, that's all I ask."

"Go away, please."

"Liana, wait. I wrote a poem for you."

He stumbled toward the stairs, but Josée blocked his way. "You heard her," she said.

He noticed, huddled in the doorway to the kitchen, Liana's half-sisters, nine-year-old twins. They stared at him wide-eyed.

"Li, please. Come outside—"

"I told you to leave!" She pushed past her mother, tugging at something on her wrist.

Then a flash of color as a bracelet winged by his head and exploded against the door. Metal beads pelted the front of his shirt, zinged off his forehead.

He backed up, and the door slammed in his face. He stood on the lawn for a moment then walked to his car like a shell-shocked private.

He hadn't seen her since.

Now he balled up the poem, tossed it into the wastebasket. Behind him, Lulu looked on, her crimson eyes afire with approval.

Six years of good memories, and all that mattered was that terrible ending.

CHAPTER 7

That evening, his brother Mark showed up clutching a Bible.

Physically, he had the worst of both worlds: a scrawny ectomorph's frame and a pot belly. He was an inch shorter than Cord with thin, colorless lips, narrow eyes. A curly-wet lock of black hair dribbled onto his forehead, evading Mark's best efforts to tuck it to the side.

Mark pointed toward Cord's bruised face. "Does your jaw click when you talk?"

Cord rubbed his mouth. For a psychotic delusion, the Coroner hit pretty damn hard. "I've got Vic's funeral tomorrow."

"I'm sorry I can't go. I have a meeting. Did you get a chance to fix Pop's headstone?"

"Rusty did." Mark had paid a fortune for the funeral, buying the most expensive headstone in the lot. But Mark could afford it. He worked in finance in the city, lived in a two-story, four-bedroom new-rise Colonial in Westchester.

"Someone left a photo of Mercy on Pop's headstone. A photo from my fight with Vic."

Mark stared at Cord in that impassive way of his. "I didn't put it there."

"But you were there, at the grave. Didn't you see it?"

"All I saw was the headstone, knocked to the ground."

Cord said, almost to himself, "Afterward, the picture faded, like it wasn't there at all. I'm not even sure I really saw it."

A look of concern crossed Mark's brow. "Are you feeling all right?"

"Now that you mention it, no, I'm not."

"Listen, Dean. I've been praying for you for quite a while now—"

"Praying for what, exactly, Mark?"

"For you to find your way. I had my own fixations when I was a child. With weapons, to be specific. With hypnotism. All that was wasteful. Sinful. But I found salvation, and I pray that you will, too. That you'll stop this fighting. Have you taken a good look in the mirror lately?"

"I don't need—"

"Victor's dead. He was your best friend."

"I know." Arguing with Mark was like arguing with a mannequin.

"Do you remember the fight you had with Pop about

your career? His health went downhill after that, fast."

"I didn't start that argument. That was Pop—"

"All right." Mark swept the stray curl off his forehead. It sprang back and hung in his face. He moved forward and eyed the fish tank glass. Lulu regarded him warily, her fuchsia tail fanning back and forth. "'The eye that mocks a father and scorns to obey a mother will be picked out by the ravens of the valley and eaten by the vultures.'"

"You've quoted that one about ten times recently. *Proverbs 30:17*."

Mark flicked the glass with his finger, and Lulu went bonkers—looping through the water in circles, her normally angular fins flattened out like dog's ears, catfish whiskers parted to the side.

"Hey, jerk-off. That's a highly sensitive fish."

"May I look at the photo album Pop gave you?"

"Huh?"

"The photo album." Mark peered around the room. "God knows how you find anything in this hovel."

"Why? You're not in it." As soon as he said it, he regretted it. Mark was a pain in the ass, that was certain. But he was Cord's only family—a half-brother he hadn't known existed. Early in his marriage—two years before Cord was born—Stanley had gotten involved with a bartender from Dover Plains. Nine months later he got a phone call. She'd had a kid named Mark—Stanley's middle name. Stan didn't argue about it. He cut the woman a check and tried to forget the whole thing. She was a single mother struggling to feed a kid with another on the way. She took the money. Cord always wondered how much Stanley had paid. What was the going rate for a bastard newborn? Did the payoff erase the guilt?

Only when Barbara died did Stan acknowledge Mark. Cord had been fourteen at the time, meeting his newfound sixteen-year-old half-brother. Mark moved into the spare bedroom and started driving Cord to high school every morning. When Mark first transferred to Havilland High, he didn't fit in. Maybe it was his vacant stare or the way he moved his lips when he was alone, carrying on a conversation with someone only he could see. The jocks and cool kids considered him weak—and in the predatory environment of high school, weakness was a social death sentence.

One day, during lunch break, some kids on the lacrosse team dragged him off into the woods. Cord saw it happen and bolted after them. He reached the woods just in time to see one of the kids—a bald juicer Cord knew from the gym—uppercut Mark to the gut while two kids held him. Mark doubled over. His glasses hit the ground.

"Let him go, Trent."

"Stay out of this, Masland," Trent said. "He was eying my girl earlier in study hall. I don't stand for that shit."

"He wasn't eyeing anyone," Cord said. "It's just the way he looks."

"Yeah, well, I don't like it."

"He's my brother," Cord warned.

The pause gave him an opportunity to appraise his odds. There were six of them in all. They were all on the same lacrosse team. They would stick together. And there was Trent, the dumbest and biggest of the lot. He was a problem. A big problem. He wouldn't back down, so Cord decided to take the initiative. He threw a straight right that caught Trent in the face and sent him sprawling in the dirt.

The others froze, out of surprise more than anything else.

"Okay," said Trent, picking himself off the ground. He wiped the blood from his lip. "Not bad. Let's see what else you got."

Cord settled into his fighting stance—rear heel raised off the ground, arms at the ready, one covering his face, the other aimed at his opponent.

A voice spoke inside his head: Sifu Lao, his old martial arts instructor. *'One does not shoot a gun by aiming at random, nor throw a punch. Point weapon at target.'*

Trent squared off in a classic boxer's stance, and Cord was vaguely aware of a circle forming around them, Mark watching from somewhere behind in a state of silent shock.

Trent threw a punch that Cord easily parried. He pivot-stepped to the side and threw a corkscrew punch that smashed into Trent's temple. His knees buckled, but he steadied himself and grinned.

"Good shot," Trent said.

Then he charged, tackling Cord to the ground. On top, Trent landed a few punches and an elbow that hammered into Cord's cheek.

Cord scrambled backward and gained his feet. With

a whooping yell, Trent charged again, but this time Cord was ready. He brought his knee up just as Trent lowered his shoulder for the tackle and connected solidly with Trent's jaw. He went down, face-planting in the dirt.

"Get him!" screamed one of the others.

Cord whirled and caught the nearest kid in the knee-cap with a side-kick. The other kids stood around, unsure whether to attack or bolt.

Cord was surprised to see Trent stumbling to his feet, mad with rage, blood bubbling from his nose, now yanked sideways. That nose looked gruesome, but apparently he still had the fight left in him. Cord lunged forward and connected with a straight right to Trent's jaw. His eyes rolled back in his head—then he fell down in place, his body toppling awkwardly with his legs buckling beneath.

That's going to hurt tomorrow, Cord thought. He hauled Mark to his feet and tugged him toward the school, pausing to retrieve his broken glasses.

The next day they had to cancel lacrosse practice because Trent, the team captain, didn't show. The others said they were jumped by a gang of kids.

After that, Mark didn't have too much trouble around school.

cɔeɔ

Now, Mark stared at Cord with that absent expression. "The photo album," he said. "The pictures of my high school graduation."

Cord cocked an eyebrow. "You sure you want to celebrate high school? I always thought you sort of blocked it out."

"Please."

"Fine, whatever."

Cord pulled the album out of the closet. He opened the album to a picture of his mother at his parents' honeymoon at Lake Placid, during the Caladium Festival Car Show. In the photo, Barbara stood in front of a souped-up Fiat Topolino with her purse slung over her bare shoulder. Her dress was pulled to the side, so you could see her slip. She smiled shyly, looking like she didn't know what to do with her hands. That was Mom, Cord thought. Always along for the ride but never certain about where she was going.

Many of the pictures were from his early childhood—Cord drooling while Barbara stuffed a greenish heap of baby food into his mouth; fishing by the lake with Mercy; in his Little League uniform, making a nice running catch in left field. There were plenty of shots of his mother: clapping in the stands, hi-fiving the other bleacher moms, and even one of her at home plate, jawing at the ump for calling Cord out—if there was one thing that got her going, it was a bad call.

And then there was his favorite picture: being carried off the field by his teammates after clocking a grand slam in the last inning to win the final game of his Little League career.

"There's not a single picture of Pop," Mark complained.

"Not surprising."

Stanley wasn't into Cord's Little League games, martial arts classes, saxophone lessons, or any other activities for that matter. Stan had stayed home, drinking beer on the porch, telling himself there must be something wrong with the world because there wasn't anything wrong with him. Sometimes Cord wasn't sure who got the better end of the deal—Mark, who grew up without a father, or Cord, who'd had such a shitty one. At least Mark hadn't had to deal with the old man's abuse for the first sixteen years of his life. But nothing either of them would do in life would ever amount to much in their father's eyes.

"Turn to the end," Mark said. Sweat dripped from his brow onto the album.

Cord wiped the vinyl with his sleeve. "You ever think about getting treatment for that?"

"I am getting treatment—hyperhidrosis therapy. They want to cauterize my sweat glands. I'm not quite there yet."

"I'd get there."

"Look," Mark said, pointing. "See?"

Cord was surprised to see a picture of Mark in a navy-blue gown, square hat, yellow tassel.

"I graduated in two-thousand-three. It seems like forever ago."

"I didn't realize Pop stuck those pictures in here," Cord said.

"He didn't. I did."

"Why?"

Mark shook his head. "You sure peaked early. Hitting home runs, everyone cheering for you. All that's behind you."

"Yeah, and you're working for Goldman Sachs. It evens out."

"Pop chose you over me."

"Pop didn't *choose* either of us. He was out for himself."

"You got all the glory. And yet I'm the success. That's paradoxical, no?"

"Don't you mean ironic?"

"'Blessed is the man that walketh not in the counsel of the ungodly, nor standeth in the way of sinners, nor sitteth in the seat of the scornful,'" Mark quoted. "'He shall be like a tree planted by the rivers of water, that bringeth forth his fruit in his season; his leaf also shall not wither; and whatsoever he doeth shall prosper.'"

Cord had the urge to grab that lock of hair and yank it out by the roots. He closed the book. "That's enough memory lane for today, bro."

Mark reopened the album to the Little League photos. Before Cord could object, Mark snatched the home-run photo out of its plastic holder. "Look here," he said.

He twirled the photo between his fingers like a magician passing a coin across his knuckles. The revolutions of the photo quickened, blurring between Mark's fingers.

Cord stared, open-mouthed. "How are you doing that?"

"Watch, brother."

"Gimme that." Cord moved to grab the photo, and a

strange thing happened. His leg muscles cramped, and he fell to the floor. He was unable to move.

Mark crouched over him, inches from his face. "Have you ever wondered why your life went downhill?"

"My legs," Cord groaned. "I can't move. Give me a hand—"

"First Liana, now Victor's death. Your life is the pits, brother."

Cord's legs spasmed, sending bolts of pain through his core. "Little help here, bro."

"I'm going to take this with me." Mark stuffed the photo in his jacket pocket. "'Destruction cometh; and they shall seek peace, and there shall be none.'"

He winked and left the room. It took Cord a few minutes to get off the floor. He felt his leg, massaging the muscles from foot to thigh. The pain was gone. He looked out to the driveway. So was his brother.

CHAPTER 8

After his brother left, Cord heard a soft whimper, like a dog crying at the back door. He followed the sound to the kitchen. Leonidas whirred by, ears flattened to his skull. His claws scrabbled for purchase on the hardwood, caught, and then he flew into Lovie's room. Cord heard it stronger now, the low moan.

The sound was coming from the basement. Cord flipped on the light, but the bulb had burned out long ago. *Typical*, he thought, wincing. He felt a migraine coming on, and it would be a bitch. He descended the basement steps in darkness, clutching the railing. "Lovie? You down here?"

The basement smelled like mothballs, moldy earth, and rat droppings. He knew the outlines of the furnace room and advanced with his arms held out in front of him. Then something grabbed his leg. He screamed, skittering backward.

"*Help me.*"

He found the light string and pulled. Lovie lay on the floor, his back turned. Cord knelt and put a hand to his side and saw the rusty puddle of blood pooling out from Lovie's nose.

"Lovie, what happened?"

"It hurts. Make it stop."

Lovie's nose was broken, Cord saw instantly. And he knew exactly what to do. As a cage fighter without health insurance, you learned how to snap bones back into place rather than going to the hospital.

"Hold still." He laid his hands across Lovie's cheek-bones and placed his thumbs on the opposite sides of his nose, against the bridge. "You with me?"

Lovie trembled, eyes tightly closed, but Cord took it as a nod.

"Don't move." He pressed harder and jerked hard to the right. There was the audible *snap* and the feeling of cartilage sliding into place under his fingers. Lovie screamed. Blood streamed out and down onto his shirt. "Better?"

Lovie nodded. "Help me up."

"What are you doing down here?"

Cord led him up the stairs. Lovie was pale as marble, his sweaty-black hair hanging in his face. One eye fluttered open, the other remained closed. "What happened to your eye, Lovie? Can you see?"

Lovie forced open his other eye. Cord stared in disbelief. The eye was filmed over in a bluish-white cataract.

Lovie's good eye rolled in its socket as if alarmed at its proximity to the damaged eye. "Everything's cloudy."

"What happened?"

Lovie stared at him, the filmy-white eye unblinking. "I heard something in the basement. When I went down there, I saw someone. He moved at me fast, hit me with something. It hurt right here," he said, pointing to his eye. "I don't even remember hitting the floor."

"Who was it?"

He wobbled like a punch-drunk fighter. "Take me to the hospital."

Cord steadied him. He inspected Lovie's watery eye, which looked like a child's bleached marble. There was a black design across the pupil:

$$死$$

"Jesus Christ. I don't believe it."

"What?"

Cord led him to the door. "Nothing."

Cord raced along the back roads, winding through the hills that lined the east bank of the Hudson. The trees pressed in tight. The ground sloped away toward the river on one side and the creek on the other. Thick clouds spattered the road with an intermittent drizzle, coating the windshield with mist. "Hold on, Lovie. We'll be there soon."

Lovie grabbed his arm. "Look out!"

At the same moment, Cord saw it—a figure in the road. That terrible face—the wild beard, crazy hair.

Those eyes. It was the same giant in his white lab coat. Cord jammed on the brakes, sending the car fishtailing. The wheels dug into dirt by the roadside, and he feared they might roll down the embankment, but he eased off the brake then counter-steered when he felt the wheels locking. The car shuddered to a stop an inch or two in front of the Coroner, who raised his hands like a third base coach holding the runner.

"Holy shit," Lovie said. "Where did he come from?"

"Get out and ask him."

"Forget that. Drive right over the fucker if he won't move."

Not a bad idea, Cord figured. But when the wipers cleared away the rain, the Coroner was gone.

 handle

At Brookhaven Hospital, Lovie looked gaunt. The cataract-eye seemed to blink in accordance with the will of some alien force.

"What did you see in the basement?

"I don't know."

"Was it the same guy from in the road?"

"I can't say."

"You can't, or you won't?"

Lovie shrugged.

"Look, someone is trying to kill me and maybe you too, now. You've got to tell me what you saw. Either that, or I'm losing my mind."

Lovie puffed out his lower lip and tucked the upper

lip in. Cord hadn't seen that expression since they were freshmen at Pace, the year Lovie got dumped by Mindy Shepherd—Pace Debate Team captain, a girl who could recite the bylaws of the American Parliamentary Debate Association in its entirety, on cue. No one knew why she bothered with Lovie in the first place, but she didn't last long. She moved on to the president of the Harvard Debate Club before six months, leaving Lovie to spend the next two years moping—writing love letters he never mailed, baking her cookies he ended up eating himself. Thus: the nickname. He put on seventy pounds but learned to tuck his upper lip every time he felt himself wanting to talk about her—it meant *keep your mouth shut, Lovie*.

"Listen, Lovie. Don't go Mindy Shepherd on me, you prick. I could be dead in three days, according to this." Cord pointed at the back of his neck.

"What the fuck is that?"

"Read it, asshole. It's my expiration date."

"Damn, Dean. All you do is think of yourself. Look at my eye, you dickhead."

What was it with people calling him *Dean* lately?

Cord glanced around the waiting room. It was nearly empty, only a mother and father waiting in a corner with a weepy child splayed across their laps and a dazed woman sitting with a bandage wrapped around her head. She glared at him, like the eyes of a Rembrandt self-portrait, her mouth half-open.

"Okay," Lovie whispered. "I'll tell you. The guy in the road, I could only see him out of this eye. The bad one. Which is weird, because I can't see shit out of it right now."

"What did he look like?"

"Like a lumberjack in a lab coat."

A nurse blared into the room: "Fred Gaines?"

"Thank God," Lovie said.

Cord followed him to the double doors, but the nurse held out a hand. "Are you a family member?" When he shook his head, she said, "Sorry, you'll have to wait here."

He slouched into a seat. He tried reading a *Sports Illustrated* but threw it back on the table with the others. He watched the minute hand on the wall clock inch toward the half-hour. The bandaged woman kept up her glare, and he shifted in the bucket seat to turn away. After a while he drifted into a doze.

Would it be so bad to take a vacation? he wondered. *To skip town and leave everything behind, like luggage fallen out over the Atlantic or stowed on the wrong flight?*

When he opened his eyes, the dazed-looking woman stood inches from him, her features waxen and rigid. The bandage around her head had come loose. It dangled in her face, blood-soaked at the tip. "On the seventh day God rested," she told him.

He shrank back in the chair. "Thanks for the update."

"I feel death, here," she said, cupping her hands over her heart. "And here."

With dismay, Cord saw her hands moving down to her crotch.

"Lady," he said, "the psych ward's in the east wing."

The woman's fingers lingered on her crotch, her mouth hanging open. Her voice deepened to a baritone. "God's work, Dean."

"What did you say?"

"Your life is a tragedy." Her voice came out like a badly dubbed foreign film: the lip movements didn't match the words. "Are you ready to embrace the Lord?"

"Embrace the Lord? I'm ready for L. Ron Hubbard right now."

"Don't take the Lord's name lightly. You're a sinner. Liana's a sinner, too."

"I haven't seen Liana in two years," he told the woman, not even sure he was speaking.

The woman lowered her head, bored into him with her rheumy glare. "'In God I trust; I will not be afraid. What can mortal man do to me?'"

Lovie snapped fingers near his ear. "Hey, Cord, wake up."

Disoriented, Cord turned as the woman retreated to her seat.

Lovie wore a patch over his damaged eye. His nose was swollen but straight.

Cord shook his head. "What'd the doctor say?"

"He said it looks like a cataract, which doesn't make sense because they don't pop up overnight. Plus, I'm too young for a cataract. He gave me some drops and a prescription. And he wants me to wear this patch for a week. How do I look?"

"Did you tell him about the guy in the road?"

"What guy?"

"What you saw, Lovie. You told me you—"

Lovie shook his head. "All I saw was rain." He stopped in front of a vending machine. "Ranch Doritos. Cool. You got a dollar?"

Cord turned back to the waiting room to see if the crazy lady would follow them, but there was no one there. The waiting room was empty.

೧೦೮೦

At home in bed, Cord lay awake, staring at the ceiling in the dark. There was something tugging at him, a memory he hadn't been willing to commit to. It lay unconfirmed, a nebulous imprint on his unconscious. After all, this hadn't been the first time he'd experienced the supernatural, but the other time had everything to do with Liana, and he'd only spent the last two years cutting her from his memory, pretending her away like a twisted dream. As he drifted off to sleep, though, his last thought was of a lake—a lake of golden jewels and a promise made to be broken...

CHAPTER 9

Summer 2009:

"Is this where you got the nickname?" Liana said. "Corduroy?"

They drove past his childhood house, a boxy Cape Cod with gabled upstairs windows and a thin, antenna-like chimney in the center. Without the chimney, the house resembled the green Monopoly house. He grew up thinking Parker Brothers designed the game piece after their home. He had a Scottish terrier named Dolly that looked suspiciously like the dog piece from the game; the street he lived on: St. James Place.

"Not here."

"But you were conceived here?"

"They lived here when I was born, but who knows, it might've been in the back of the Chevelle."

"Your parents were probably too prudish for that. I'd

bet good money it was missionary-style in the parental lair. I'd bet you were conceived around seven p.m. Your dad goes to bed early."

"He does. You can get the details from him when you see him."

She laughed. "Maybe I will."

They parked in front of a playground on the eastern edge of the lake with the windows down, watching a few kids tumble down the slides shaped like tentacles of a huge octopus.

The head of the monster reared up ten feet off the ground, with a hole in the mouth where the kids slid down into its belly, a spongy central core made of foam. The octopus had bulging Mr. Potato Head eyes, but one black pupil had fallen off, leaving a gaping white hole on that side.

"There aren't enough cephalopodic playgrounds in this country. The mollusk class, in general, is wholly misrepresented in jungle gyms, don't you think?"

"I hadn't given it much thought."

"That's your problem," she said. "You don't think enough about the important things in life."

A boy in a red pair of overalls tumbled hard off the bottom slide and landed in the dirt. The child's face crumpled, and he let out a hitching wail, prompting his mother to come running to pick him up. Before long, the kid scissored his legs to be put down then ran back to the slide.

"What are your thoughts on these urchins?" she asked. "Do you like them?"

"In theory, yes. But I might not be well-suited for parenting."

"How so?"

"Let's say the kid came home one day with a principal's note saying he was fighting in school. I'd be excited for him, if he won. And if not, I'd want to show him some moves."

Liana frowned. "Well, that makes two of us. I'd be a terrible mother."

"Why do you say that?"

"I'd be playing a different role every other night. The kid would be a bipolar disorder waiting to happen."

"You'd be great."

She shook her head as if expressing a great sorrow. "Years of therapy. She'd grow up watching *True Blood* reruns and get skanky vampire tattoos, with black nail polish and hoops through her nasal cartilage." She paused, then recited: "'O comfort-killing night, image of hell, dim register and notary of shame, black stage for tragedies and murders fell, vast sin-concealing chaos, nurse of blame.'"

"That's what I love about you," he said. "Your shining optimism." They walked down Tom Collins Avenue toward Sterling Lake.

"So, you think you'll ever grow out of this fighting thing?"

He shrugged. "I don't really see it as a *thing* to grow out of."

"Your idea of fun is rolling around on a canvas with sweaty men? How's a girl supposed to feel about that?"

"Supportive?"

She gave him a sideways look, the wind blowing her hair across her eyes. "Why do you do it?"

"Why do you act?"

"I like it. I'm good at it."

"Is that all?"

"It's a compulsion."

"'Every form of addiction is bad, no matter whether the narcotic be alcohol or morphine or idealism.'" He studied her face, saw her eyes widen momentarily. "You're not the only one who knows Jung."

"Sometimes you surprise me, Mr. Masland," she said. "*Dean.*"

He smiled. It was rare that he "won" these verbal battles, so he reveled in each small victory, like an Arizona farmer finally seeing the skies darken for rain.

"I feel sorry for my mother."

"Your mother?"

"I'm thinking about how she'll react when I tell her what you do for a living."

"Tell her Mike Tyson got ten million for a fight."

"She probably won't know who that is."

By May the campground was open, but it didn't get crowded until Memorial Day, so they had the lake to themselves.

The water was sparkling bright, the sunlight painting a path of gold jewels onto the surface from one bank to the other, two miles across. Liana walked to the edge and kicked off her sandals. He caught her toeing the ripples in the water, cocking her head to the side. Cord liked watching her. On stage, in real life. Was there any difference?

Suddenly, she made a move to step in. He grabbed her arm. "Water's freezing."

"I wasn't going to go in, I was going to go *on*. Can't you see the path?"

"That's something I'd pay to see."

"How much?"

He took out his wallet. "My last dollar."

"Okay, a dollar then."

"Deal." He tried to tuck the dollar into the waistband of her jeans, but she danced away, laughing.

"Not yet. Give it to me after."

"Fine, but there's something I want you to have now."

"And what would that be?"

He pulled out a silver beaded bracelet he'd bought for her. He'd saved up two months to get it, was proud of the purchase, even though two months' grave-digging wages wasn't exactly a fortune. "It's not much," he said, "but it's from the heart."

"It's beautiful." She held out her wrist. "Put it on me." He slipped on the bracelet.

She smiled and looked out over the water. Then her gaze hardened, the smile leaking from her face.

"Li? You okay?"

She shook it off like a cold shiver. "Yes," she said, her smile returning. "Fine."

He watched as she took off her T-shirt, unbuckled her belt, wriggled her jeans past her hips. Her skin was cream-white, in sharp contrast to her lacy black bra and panties, dark auburn hair. As summer dug in and she spent more time in the sun, her hair would turn a light tawny brown, but right then it was still dark, wavy dark.

"Do you see anything you like?"

He glanced around to make sure they were alone, sheltered by overhanging oaks and a dense copse of brambly bushes and weeping willows. *I bet there's a bed of needles under one of those willows*, he thought.

She followed his gaze, holding her arms across her breasts, shivering slightly in the cool breeze. "I know what you're thinking, you bad boy. Get those dirty thoughts out of your mind, this is serious business."

"Okay, fine. Who are you this time, the Lady of the Lake?"

"No, silly. She came *out* of the water. I'm going to *cross* it."

"Well, go ahead."

She paused. "The price of admission just went up. A dollar and a promise."

"What promise?"

"After. Right now you have to close your eyes and hold out your arms like you're flying."

"Then how will I know—"

She put her hands on her hips, shot him an impatient look.

"Fine." He closed his eyes, held out his arms. One thing he knew about Liana—arguing with her was point-less, like a stare-down with a wall.

"No peeking."

"I'm not."

"I need you to help me visualize the trail of gold across the water."

"Okay, Dorothy."

He felt a light tap on his forehead. He didn't realize she was that close. "Focus, Corduroy," she said, her voice slowly moving away. "And keep your eyes closed. This is important stuff here."

He sighed and kept his eyes closed. Despite the chill in the air, the sun felt hot on his face. His arms grew tired from holding the pose.

"You're not picturing it," she complained. Her voice seemed to come from a distance. The water's edge was maybe ten feet away. *What the hell?*

He did what she said, pictured the gold flecks on the water, their liquid undulations. He saw them solidifying, linked together like the iron mesh of a security gate—something you could walk on, a solid path of sparkling gems.

He heard her laugh, echoing off the water, brought back by the cold wind. "That's it, Corduroy. Almost there." Her voice was faint, as if he heard the words inside his head. He felt dizzy, like he was a kid again, spinning on the old tire Stanley had hung from the oak in their front yard a half-mile from here.

Maybe it was still there. You got on and someone wound the rope—tighter and tighter, until the cord bunched up and knotted above—then let it go as you unwound through space, centripetal forces laying siege to your nervous system. When you got off, you took a step and fell face-first onto the grass, laughter surging through your gut. That was how he felt—an eight-year-old coming down off that tire.

"Look now, Corduroy."

His eyes snapped open, and what he saw drove the air from his lungs. Liana stood on the sunlit path of water, arms held out from her sides for balance. He blinked and she was gone, a gush of water rushing to fill the empty space. He jumped up. "Liana!"

Her head bobbed to the surface, and she drew in a breath. She was ten feet out and already deep in over her head. The lake was built from a quarry that they'd flooded in the 1930s, all deep water, hardly any shallows. Cord dove in, hitting the water and power stroking toward her. The frigid water paralyzed his muscles. He slipped an arm around her waist and hauled her to the surface, backstroking until his feet finally touched the craggy bottom. She made a strangled sound in his ear as he carried her out of the water. It took him a moment to realize she was laughing.

"Can't you swim?" he said, eyes bugging.

She coughed into the back of her hand, choked out another burst of laughter. "The sun went behind the clouds. Did you see?"

"Liana, I don't know *what* I saw."

"You saw." She held out her hand, palm up. "I believe we agreed on a dollar. And a promise."

TWO Days...

CHAPTER 10

Attention MMA fans, this is the event you've all been waiting for: the first annual Fight Like Hell amateur tournament. Don't miss your favorite underground fighters in bone-crunching action this Thursday, April fifteenth, at the New Jersey Civic Center in Edison. Call Ticketmaster to reserve your seat for this soon-to-be-sold-out event—"

გადავ

Half-delirious from sleep, Cord threw out an arm, swatted the alarm clock to the floor. He swung his legs out of bed and stomped the device with the heel of his foot. It gave out an electronic whimper and was silent. *Oh, well,* he thought. *Thing was on the fritz anyway.*

On the way downstairs, he passed Senator's room. Senator lay on the bed, smothering his face with a pillow, his body racked with sobs. Whatever the cause of Senator's problem, Cord didn't much care. He had other things on his mind: Mercy's funeral, for one. He figured that alone excluded him from having to deal with Senator today.

"Corduroy? Is that you?"

Ah, shit, he thought. "It's me, buddy. What's wrong?"

Senator's bedroom looked like a seventies porno set: shag rug, a gold Buddha languishing on a dresser, ruffled throw pillows with braided-rope accents, lava lamp. An overgrown Chamaedorea wisped out of the corner, evoking West Palm Beach. Senator kept Tarot cards in three separate decks on his desk: *The Pool*, *Fate*, and *Aloneness*. He liked to give readings to his romantic interests, his own little seduction trick.

Senator wore his pinstriped Savile Row from the night before, now rumpled and creased in the wrong spots. A nametag was pinned to the lapel:

John Valor, Republican—CT. "Team Valor."

He held his arms out like a mewling child waiting to be picked up. Cord patted him on the back.

"Did you see the front page?" Senator nodded toward the bed, where Leonidas lay in a crumpled pile of newspapers.

"Did the cat piss on your newspaper again?"

"No. It's *awful*."

Cord grabbed for the paper, but Leonidas hissed and swatted at his hand. "That's a good kitty," he said, feinting at the paper's edge. Leonidas bit on the fake, boxed at the air while Cord came around the back and yanked. The cat tumbled off the bed, landing on its feet and sprinting out of the room.

Cord unfolded the front page: *Valor Indicted in Underage Prostitution Ring.*

Cord had met the Congressman a few times. When Cord went to shake hands, his hand had been not so much shaken as engulfed. The Congressman had an easy, rolling laugh that made you feel all was well in the world. He was a hardline Christian conservative, against gay marriage, immigration, and abortion. On sensitive topics, he deferred to the Bible.

"Last night I came out to my father."

"Are you serious?"

Senator nodded. "I didn't want to say anything at the table, so I followed him into the bathroom."

"You told your dad while you were pissing?"

"He was in the stall, actually. I was outside the door."

"What happened?"

"I underestimated his reaction. He charged out like a bull and tackled me. We wrestled around on the bathroom floor until a couple of cops came in looking for him. Next thing I knew, they had him in handcuffs and were reading him his rights before he had his pants buckled." He howled in agony. "Prostitution and young girls, Cord."

"Gee, Senator," Cord said. "That's tough. We're here for you, though, me and Lovie."

He looked up, saucer-eyes glistening, hopeful.

At that moment, Lovie appeared in the doorway,

wearing a leopard-print coat and a purple boa. "Hey, Senator, I bought this for your daddy. Thought he might like to wear it on the way to Sing-Sing."

This caused Senator to break out in a fresh volley of sobs.

❧❦❧

On the way to Mercy's funeral, Cord detoured toward Mark's house. He needed an explanation. What had happened yesterday? Mark's visit, the resulting sickness. Mark had been acting funny these last few days—right around the time the Coroner showed up. He had always been a loose screw. Growing up, he'd been impossible to read. Cord never understood his motivations. But Mark didn't seem capable of this level of sadism. And Cord didn't have anything to do with him being a bastard. He'd always treated him like a brother.

Then Cord thought of Jade, Mark's wife. They certainly made an odd pair. She was a Wiccan, an occultist. For as long as Cord could remember, Mark had been rooting for her to convert, but maybe she'd finally corrupted him. Cord pictured her drawing her arcane figures, lighting her candles. He had never taken her witchcraft seriously—who would? But he'd seen some things over the past few days—*the past few years, really*, he thought, remembering Liana at the lake—that made the supernatural seem more than plausible.

Half a mile from Mark's house, Cord felt his gut cramping. He'd had a cup of Senator's coffee that morning, but his stomach was used to that napalm. It was the same sickening pain from yesterday, when Mark held that photo. Bile rose in the back of Cord's throat as he pulled into a vacant lot. There, he vomited on the pavement then sat back and sucked in deep gasps of air. Usually, throwing up made him feel better—it had done the trick before many of his early fights. Not now, though. He still felt as if he might puke again. Delirious, he drove half a mile in the opposite direction, until he finally began to feel better. The knot in his stomach began to unwind.

He dialed Mark. Voicemail, first ring. He snapped shut the phone and fired it at the passenger seat. He drew in a deep breath. *Get to the funeral*, he thought. *Then deal with Mark.* He inspected his black suit, looking for splashes of vomit. It looked fine.

He checked his watch. He didn't have much time.

CHAPTER 11

Woodside Cemetery. Odd to be here in daylight, Cord thought.

He parked in his customary spot in front of the garage, next to Father Reginald's Prius, which bore a bumper sticker with the message *Christians aren't perfect, just forgiven.* Dark clouds bowed low in the sky, breeding a drizzly mist. Cord couldn't see beyond the cemetery's boundaries, just a sliver of gray fencing. A kid was directing mourners to park up the hill near Moog's funeral home and Holy Reckoning Church, where Father Reginald would perform the service.

In the garage, Cord came upon Rusty, rolling on a mechanic's creeper beneath the huge backhoe they used for excavating the Willow's Corner bedrock. Rusty's teeth worked over a blade of barley grass that protruded from the corner of his mouth.

He always seemed to be chewing on something. It

was no wonder his teeth had worn down to yellow nubs.

"Need some help?"

"You're not dressed to be no grease monkey. And you got a funeral to go to."

"I got time," Cord said, not in any hurry to head up to the church.

"I can't find a single thing wrong with this machine. Damn thing just won't run," complained Rusty. "I wish your daddy was around. That man could fix one of these monsters just by looking at it. He never studied mechanics a day in his life, but it made sense to him anyway. Best mechanic I ever knew. He used to lend a hand around the orchard, fixin' the speed-sprayers and such. You and your brother used to come out now and again. You was in your teens then, you remember?"

Cord nodded. Stanley sometimes brought Mark and him to the orchard to "help out," but mostly they ran around shooting each other with paint guns, Mark's idea.

As if channeling his thoughts, Rusty said, "I tell ya something else, too. That man was a dead shot at a hundred yards."

Stan liked guns. He had a Winchester Model 70 and a .22 bolt action. If it moved and was legal to shoot, Stan believed it to be fair game. He liked pointing out that he was a better shot than Mark.

He always ran Mark down, every chance he got. He'd had it against him from the moment he arrived at their doorstep, a sixteen-year-old kid with a couple of dead parents and a suitcase. And who could blame the old man? He had forked over a sizable sum to pretend Mark away—and yet he'd returned, the prodigal bastard.

"There was that time with the groundhogs. You remember that?"

The groundhogs. Cord noticed his reflection in the window. The gash on the bridge of his nose looked ragged, its color deepening to a purplish-blue. The mouse under his eye had yellowed, the color smeared across his cheek like a dirt stain. He had an abrasion on his jaw. It still hurt to move it sideways.

"You okay, Cord? You look a little pale."

One morning Stan had appeared with his two rifles, asking the boys if they were ready to hunt some marsupials. The old man didn't seem to know that groundhogs were not marsupials, and Cord wasn't going to enlighten him.

They took the rifles—Cord the Winchester, Mark the .22—to the orchard near Rusty's shop, where the groundhogs had dug trenches underneath the apple trees, cutting off the roots.

"Put your head to the ground and listen," said Stan. "They're in there all right."

Cord did as his father instructed. He could hear the animals deep in the burrow, a sound like the earth breathing.

"I'll get one, Dad," Mark said with a wild look in his eye. "You watch."

When the first groundhog came out of its hole, Stan shot it in the head, point blank. All that remained was a furry, headless corpse, chunks of bone and gristle smeared through wiry tufts of orchard grass.

"Geez, Dad," Mark squealed. "You really nailed that one."

It wasn't the blood and gore but the smell of burned flesh and fur that made Cord ill.

Mark winged the next one. His poor eyesight made him a bad shot, and the groundhog limped off on three legs. Mark raised his arms. "Told you I'd get one!"

The groundhog dragged itself back to its hole, trailing blood on the grass. This time, when Cord put his ear to the ground, he heard something different—whimpering, like a small child trapped somewhere deep.

"No bawling now, you hear?"

"Yeah, Dean," Mark pitched in. "Leave the shooting to me and Dad."

They stayed all afternoon, the air rich with gunpowder, the ground awash in blood and gore. Those furry bodies, the floppy tails—all piled where his father instructed. One was still moving, Cord noticed. A baby one, twitching its foot. This time, Cord couldn't hold back his tears.

CHAPTER 12

Holy Reckoning featured modern Roman Catholic architecture—steeple in the foreground with a starburst window set like an eye in the center, peaked stained glass windows, white siding. Inside, the nave aisle intersected the transept at the crossing, the sanctuary with a raised altar, choir lofts on either side, punctuated by an effigy of Christ on the cross. The wooden pulpit—draped in red velvet—rose to the left forefront of the sanctuary, situated between opposing flights of stairs. Father Reginald, a bald man stooped by age, hovered above the dais, trailing sacramental vestments over his bony arms.

The church seated about a hundred people. Today, it pushed past maximum capacity, standing room only in the rear. Behind Cord the doors banged shut with a loud report as sudden as a gunshot. Half the congregation turned, making him feel like a gatecrasher.

Father Reginald droned, "'The Lord is my shepherd; I shall not want...'" He always delivered *Psalm 23* to end the proceedings. "'Surely goodness and mercy will follow me all the days of my life, and I will dwell in the house of the Lord forever.'"

Cord stood in the corner underneath a mural of *The Last Supper*, breathing incense and acanthaceae mint. He recognized some faces in the crowd—Bodie Walker, Andre Lot, and a bunch of other MMA fighters from the gym. Mercy's aunt and her four adopted kids sat in the front, alongside a few of his cousins and his ninety-year-old grandmother. Kelly sat in the middle, staring straight ahead. Senator was in the front row, too, dabbing at his eyes with a hanky. Lovie sat next to him, craning his neck to ogle a redhead in the third pew with his good eye. Cord wondered if this many people would show up for his funeral. He doubted it. He didn't think he even knew *fifty* people, let alone enough to fill a church.

He thought of his father's funeral and its meager turnout: Mark and Rusty and an old man who'd worked with Stan at the shop who smelled like whiskey and motor oil. Later, a small group arrived at Stanley's grave. Liana had placed a flower on the casket: a lone rose. Cord, no stranger to the task, had heaved the first shovelful of dirt; then Mark followed, the soil hitting the lid of the coffin with a hollow thud. For Cord, the tears wouldn't come. No one could muster any tears that day. Not surprising, Cord thought. Stanley had inspired little emotion in life; why now in death?

Now, Father Reginald finished up by passing out

white processional candles with paper bobeches as drip protectors. An usher handed Cord a candle. An altar boy traveled up the aisle with a lit taper, igniting the wicks of those close by, who ignited others in turn. In a few minutes, the flame had worked its way to Cord and the other latecomers in the back.

Reginald held up his hands to quiet the congregation. "Let this flame be symbolic of our eternal love for one another, but be aware that like all love, it often burns. Hold it upright, not sideways." After all the candles were lit, Father Reginald said, "Jessica and Andy, if you would do the honors."

A shudder rippled through the congregation as the lights went out. Even with the hundred odd lit candles, Holy Reckoning was dark. From the rear of the church, Reginald looked like a low-budget apparition drifting out over the parish.

A large candelabrum came to life as an altar boy stood on the dais with a long pointer, igniting the ornamental candles.

"Now let us share a moment of silence for our dear departed friend, Victor Mercy."

Everyone bowed their heads in the flickering candlelight. Cord closed his eyes and mouthed the words of Percy Bysshe Shelley. "'He has outsoared the shadow of our night, envy and calumny and hate and pain, and that unrest which men miscall delight, can touch him not and torture not again.'"

When he opened his eyes, his candle had blown out. There was a draft in the back. He pushed away from the wall as a black figure, a woman, came toward him holding a candle.

"Cord," she whispered. "Hold still."

She turned her candle sideways—spilling a single drop of wax onto the floor—and the wicks shared a kiss, and then the other candle retreated, leaving behind a burning flame. She moved away before he could say anything, a whisper of black melting into the gloom. He made a move to follow, but his legs locked up and he clutched the wall for balance.

When the lights snapped on, Father Reginald instructed the parishioners to continue down the hill for the burial service. Everyone rose at once, reminding Cord of CROWD, that meandering conglomerate of spectators in his nightmare. He moved to the corner, away from the throng pushing subway-style past him.

At last he saw her. She was hanging back, toward the dais. He moved down the aisle, nearly bumping into her mother, who stepped into the aisle.

"Hello, Mrs. Sénécal."

"Hello, Dean."

"How is she?"

"She's never been better. And I'd like to keep it that way."

He blew out his candle. Smoke curled up, itching his nostrils with a burn-barrel smell, the smell of a house on fire.

"I must say, Dean, this was a senseless tragedy. What were you thinking, fighting your best friend?"

He had to choke back his words. *You wouldn't un-*

derstand. You never once put your neck on the line for anything you wanted. Instead he mumbled, "It was an accident."

"An accident that took a life. Where has all this *fighting* gotten you?" Her eyes bored into him like cold bits of charcoal, saying the same thing some part of his conscience had been telling him for two days now.

"It's what I do," he said.

She snorted. "Victor didn't deserve to die like an animal in a cage."

Father Reginald came toward them, opening his arms. Josée grabbed her daughter and led her down the side aisle.

"Dear boy," the priest said, his white vestments sagging like wrinkled skin.

Cord took his hands. "Thank you for the service, Father."

"I thought you might like to take confession."

Cord shot a glance at Liana as she went out the front door. She looked back, catching his eye. "Not right now, Father."

"Yes, now," said Father Reginald, catching his arm. "This would be an ideal time for confession, I think."

"Right before the service, Father?"

"Yes, it's unconventional, certainly, but we have a little time."

Cord sighed. The Father had a point.

Reckoning was at hand.

☙☙☙

Cord had inherited a fear of confined spaces from his mom, which is why he broke into a cold sweat as soon as he sat down in the confessional booth. The size of a bathroom stall, the booth was paneled in rosewood.

He sat on a small wooden chair—probably taken from a middle school classroom—and looked across at the iron grate, behind which Reginald sat.

When Reginald cleared his throat, Cord made the sign of the cross. He noticed the plaque on the bench, which read, *Donated by Brady Valor.* Cord had to laugh.

"Forgive me Father, for I have sinned. It's been a while since my last confession." He paused. "I killed my best friend, as you know. I didn't mean to do it. Is that still a sin?"

"No, my son."

"I had sex out of wedlock. Many times. I've entertained impure thoughts and committed impure acts by myself countless times. Sometimes I go on the Internet and—"

"I understand. What else?"

"I've committed many violent acts against my fellow man, mostly in a cage, mostly for money."

"Anything else?"

"I have a friend who's gay. Is that a sin?"

"Are you yourself a homosexual?"

"No."

"Do you have impure thoughts about him?"

"No."

"Then, no. It's not a sin."

Cord racked his brain, trying to get it all out while he

could. The Father was right: his time was short. "I dislike my brother. In truth, I've never liked him. That has to be a sin."

"Cain and Abel," Reginald muttered. "Why do you hate your brother?"

"I think he may have put some kind of curse on me." Cord pulled in a deep breath. *What do I have to lose?* He turned his back to the grate but wasn't sure if Reginald could make out the tattoo in the dark.

Reginald sounded like he was yawning. "What kind of curse?"

"He's ten feet tall and has a milky white eye." Cord realized how he sounded but couldn't stop himself. It was like squeezing a pimple—you knew you shouldn't do it, but once you got started, you had to see it through. In a halting monotone, Cord told the priest everything. When he was finished, he said, "Father, I swear it's all true. Am I crazy?"

There was a long pause. "Father?" The sound of light snoring rumbled through the iron grate, echoing through the confessional chamber.

CHAPTER 13

Cord descended the hill toward Willow's Corner to the Mercy family plot. The mourners would be gathered, waiting for the casket to be brought down from the funeral home for Father Reginald's graveside service. They might have to wait a while longer, thought Cord, who hadn't bothered to disturb the priest on his way out. The old codger looked like he could use some rest. The pause would give Cord time to find Liana. She'd surprised him in church. He hadn't imagined she would be there.

Clouds were rolling in like thick swabs of filthy cotton blackened around the edges. It would rain soon. Thunder sounded in the distance, and he thought of his mother. Barbara, with her grocery list of medications, doped out of her mind. She had an aversion to electrical storms—well, storms of any kind, really. As a kid he remembered her yelling for him to come inside, that the worst place to be was playing outside during a thunderstorm. Actually, the worst place you wanted to be during a thunderstorm was in the house with her as she paced back and forth in the dark, pulling plugs on appliances and moving everything away from the nearest electrical outlet. By the time the storm was over, they had a jumbled pile of domestic devices sitting chest-high in the living room.

He suddenly had the urge to run away—anywhere would do. A Buddhist monastery, say. Maybe running was his best bet. He could buy a one-way ticket and get lost somewhere the Coroner couldn't reach him. The problem: he didn't have money for a plane ticket. Hell, he didn't have money for the laundromat.

Willow's Corner was aptly named for the copse of weeping willows brooding over a small stream at the western perimeter of the cemetery. The leaves drizzled over the bowed limbs like human tresses, reminding Cord of the hairbags he knew in high school, heavy metal kids who smoked pot in the bathroom and wore Venom T-shirts with pentagrams on the front. Willow's Corner was an expensive burial choice at upward of thirty-five hundred per plot. Where else could you get the foliage to mourn for you? Mercy's parents' life insurance policy had paid for the plot: a corner plot, ten yards from the fence.

Cord surveyed the mourners. He caught sight of Liana toward the back by the fence. Mercy's aunt, tugging along a row of kids, passed in front. One of the adopted children, the youngest, a ten-year-old girl who wore a frilly blue dress and matching buckled shoes, stopped suddenly, holding up the convoy, and stared at Cord. She placed a finger on her lower lip, cocking her head to the side. "Mommy," she said. "Is that the bad man?"

An old man blocked his path. "You're the Masland boy, ain'cha?" the man said with a yellow-toothed grin. He had liver spots on his forehead, bushy eyebrows.

"That's him," the man's wife said, appearing out of the crowd. "I never forget a face."

Cord offered his hand, which the old man vigorously pumped. Cord had met these folks before—good, honest farming people who had worked one of the local apple orchards for years before passing the business on to their children.

"You're the sumbitch who murdered Vic," the man said, still pumping his hand.

"That's him," the woman said. "I never forget—"

"This is the hand that did it, ain't it? That's some right you got."

Cord extricated his hand. "I'm sorry."

"Ain't that funny, Ma?" the man said. "We outlived our own nephew, and he's sorry. Way I see it, you should be in jail."

Cord backed away, but the man lashed out, dug his fingers into his forearm. Strong grip for a codger.

"You got some nerve showing your face here. If I were you, I'd steer clear of this congregation."

Thunder grumbled overhead. Cord felt the first drops of rain splash on his forehead.

"You're gonna pay for what you done," the man

said, saliva spritzing from between his lips. "If not in this life, then the next."

Cord shook free from the grip. "Vic was my best friend. No one feels worse than me."

"Yeah, you're all torn up, I can tell."

"You killed him," the woman said.

"If I was a few years younger," the man said, fists clenched, "I'd knock your block off."

Most of the mourners were staring at them, muttering under their breath. A light drizzle began to fall.

"Listen, I'm sorry for your loss—"

"We'd walk the orchards together," the woman interrupted, her stubbled chin trembling. "Even with that bad leg of his, he'd always climb the trees and pick the best apples and cut them into pieces for me. Sometimes I brought them home and made—"

"Respectfully, Ma," the man said, "you're not makin' sense. That wasn't Vic. You're thinking of the Robinson boy."

The woman scrunched up her face in a desperate look of confusion, one Cord knew well. He'd seen his own mother give him that look from the hospital bed the last few months of her life. Especially when her medication wasn't regulated properly or when a bad-spell sank its teeth in and bit down hard. "It's not him?"

"This here's that no-good Masland boy. His father was no good, too. I knew that sumbitch from way back…"

Cord walked on, ignoring the glares of the mourners. Dr. Kilgore, the pediatrician who'd delivered him as a baby, stood near a tall cedar. The doctor dodged his glance and wiped at an imaginary spot on his pant leg.

Over by the broken fountain, Kelly stood by herself, clutching an umbrella, her hair pulled back so tight it looked like she'd given herself a facelift. "You shouldn't have come," she said.

Cord shook his head. "I knew him better than any of these people."

"I know, but…"

"But what?"

"Well, for starters, you killed him."

Cord stared at her, the anger welling up in his gut. "That's not fair, Kelly."

"This is a time for family. And right now, these people equate you with all the mistakes Vic made."

"Fighting wasn't a goddamn mistake. If Vic didn't have MMA, he would've been in prison, or worse. It's true, and you know it."

"You might be right, Cord." She threw a sideways glance at him, her eyes pooled with tears. "But no one cares about that right now."

She fumbled open her umbrella and started down the hill. As she picked her way through the headstones, the rain began in earnest. Cord didn't own an umbrella. His one good dress shirt was soaked to the seams.

"Cord, over here!"

Liana was standing between the limbs of a willow tree. It was a shock. She looked to him like an actress in a play, like the first time he saw her onstage as Ophelia, moving with a lithe grace, talking her way through mad riddles at a collegiate production, the only person worth watching on the entire stage. He remembered the hotel room afterward, purchased with the last of his savings. There they'd turned off all the lights but the yellow one spilling out from the bathroom, slipped beneath the unfamiliar sheets, and felt each other for the first time.

Now, he ducked under a branch, parted the moisture-laden leaves, slipped through a curtain of waterlogged silk. It was surprisingly dry under the willow, whose bell shape channeled most of the rain down the tree's leafy hull. Liana leaned back against the trunk. Her hair clung to her forehead, a smudge of dirt on her black dress. She looked paler than he remembered, barefoot on the damp earth, fingernails and toes painted with black-lacquered nail polish.

For two years he'd played out this moment—what he would do when he ran into her in a grocery store or movie theater. The hurt of betrayal, the embarrassment of his longing.

Now, he stared at her, and there was no anger or hurt—only his dry throat and a tightness in his chest, making it hard to breathe. She stared at him blankly.

Finally, he broke the silence by asking, "Black nail polish? Are you going Goth on me?"

She nodded. "I'm planning on buying a pair of those plastic vampire teeth."

"You know, most people go *in*side to get out of the rain."

"I am inside," she said. "I'm hiding from my mother."

There was a long pause. He studied the grass.

"You didn't return my call."

"I thought about it." He had a grocery list of things he wanted to say to her, but his neural pathways were cooked.

"I joined this acting troupe out of Montreal," she said. "I'm thinking about moving up there."

"Good for you." His voice sounded a few decibels too high.

She sat on a bed of willow leaves. "C'mere."

"You'll get your dress dirty."

She patted the ground next to her. "Nah, this old thing. Have a seat."

He sat. They listened to the rain pattering off the leaves, which reminded Cord of getting caught in his Sterling Lake tree fort with Mercy during a storm, listening to the hollow thudding of the fat raindrops against the wood siding mixed with the soft rustle of precipitation against the foliage.

"I miss him," he said.

She slid an arm across his shoulder.

"Me, too. Don't listen to what anyone says. It's not your fault."

"I can't stop thinking about the sound of his head hitting the canvas. The way his eyes rolled back."

She used a finger to hook under his chin, point his face toward hers. He could see his tears mirrored in her eyes. When she blinked, a watery ribbon traced the curve of her cheek. "Maybe you saved him."

"Saved him?"

"Vic wanted it this way. To go out fighting."

He drew in an unsteady breath. "Ever since his death, there's been all this weird stuff happening…"

"Like what?"

"You wouldn't believe me if I told you."

"Cord," Liana began, "I have to tell you something—"

A shrill voice from nearby cut her off. She grimaced and held a finger to her lips.

Cord peered out from between the boughs. "It's your mom."

Josée strode between a row of headstones calling for her daughter. *She's got a set of pipes on her*, Cord thought. Maybe her voice would wake Father Reginald.

The rain had tapered off a bit. The crowd had regathered, and Moog had driven the hearse down from the funeral home. The pallbearers stood around, waiting to unload the coffin. Cord looked away, unprepared to view that wooden box.

"C'mon," Liana said, grabbing his hand. "Time to face the music."

He shook out of her grasp. "I can't. They think I'm a murderer, Li."

"*I* don't think that."

"You're about the only one."

Before she could protest, he retreated deeper into the depths of the tree and pushed through to the other side, moving swiftly along the fence and disappearing down the hill toward the parking lot, trailed by remorse.

ᘒᘒᘒ

A Buick Regal was parked behind his Celica. *Gallo*, he thought.

As he neared, the Buick's door opened, and Gallo slid out. With his sunglasses on despite the weather, he looked like Don Johnson from *Miami Vice*—only thirty years older and half-crippled. "How was the funeral?"

"I left early."

"Guilt will do that to you."

"I have to be somewhere," Cord said.

"I spoke to Doctor Kendall today. Mr. Mercy's physician."

Cord held up in front of his car, one hand on the door handle. "And?"

"Turns out Mercy had a brain problem. Doc Kendall prescribed medication and warned him not to fight. Said it could kill him if he did."

"No." The parking lot swam in Cord's vision. "There's no way that's true. He would've told me."

"You think the doctor is lying?"

"What does it matter what I say? You won't believe me anyway."

Gallo narrowed his eyes. He opened the notepad bulging from his front pocket.

"What about the promoter?" Cord asked. "He allowed him to fight—"

"This promoter's in legal trouble, I assure you. He allowed Mercy to participate without medical clearance. But for the moment, I'm interested in you."

"I didn't know he had a brain condition. If I did, I never would've fought him."

"Look at it my way, Mr. Masland. Let's say you had a grudge against someone. Let's say you wanted to kill him, and you knew he had a brain defect, and you also knew right where to hit him. Wouldn't that be the ideal means? All you would need to do is get him in the ring."

"It's a cage," Cord corrected.

"Well?"

"He complained about headaches," Cord said, almost to himself, "but in our line of work, you get headaches."

"I don't suppose you tried to stop him."

"Do I look like his doctor? I was his training partner."

"Is my line of questioning making you uncomfortable?"

"Go check the videotape. You'll see what happened."

"Oh, I've looked at it," he said. "I've seen your expression just before you threw that right."

"Yeah?"

"Yeah. I see hatred in your face. Sheer murderous hatred."

"Did you see me crying over his body?"

Gallo tucked his notepad into his shirt pocket. "Oh, I saw the whole thing. Robert De Niro would be proud."

"Screw off, Gallo."

"I'll do that, son. But I'll be watching you. And I'll be back. You'll fuck up sooner or later. Killers always do."

CHAPTER 14

Cord changed out of his dress clothes, bought a six-pack, and drove. He needed to clear his mind. The accusing stares from Mercy's family were seared into his memory, there every time he closed his eyes. He took a deep breath and tried to relax, but the images of Mercy's family were replaced by those of Gallo. The crotchety old fuck and his ridiculous accusations.

Why was he the only one who understood the irony? If not for him, Mercy would've been dead long ago. The highway opened before him, and the countryside melted past, and he thought of Sterling Lake and Billings Elementary and their second-grade teacher, Mrs. Jones, who, it was widely known, had ten children from three different marriages. The first thing he remembered about Mercy was the day he raised his hand in class and asked Mrs. Jones if her insides hurt from having so many kids. Seven years old and already a smartass. They spent the next few summers climbing trees and riding bikes. Mercy had liked to pull pranks. One time he loosened the lug nuts on the tires of a neighbor's bike, and the next day they watched in awe as the wheel fell off, spilling the kid over the handlebars and to the ground, like some clown in a circus stunt. He ended up in the hospital, broken collarbone.

Mercy's mom died when he was little, and his dad had heavy hands. He'd even broken Mercy's jaw once. Eventually, Mercy learned to fight back. After that, he was always fighting. He busted a classmate's nose because he thought the kid was staring at him funny. It turned out the kid was blind. There were other stories, Cord thought. Worse ones. Mercy's suicide attempt. Or, in juvie, how some kid buried a sharpened spoon five inches into his gut. There was an older kid who tried to fondle him. Mercy had choked him unconscious.

And of course, there was the house fire. How could Cord forget? He was thirteen, the year before his mother died. On the way to Vic's house, he'd smelled something other than the lake water and swamp. A burn barrel smell. As he got closer, there was red light over the trees and smoke curling upward. When he arrived, the fire had already spread to the second level, with flames shooting out of the roof and windows. A huge oak near the house was on fire, looking like the Statue of Liberty's torch. Mercy's dog came running from around back, barking like mad. When Cord saw it, he knew Mercy was still inside. He already felt the heat over his body, like reaching into an oven. He grabbed a beach towel on the grass, damp from the lawn sprinklers. He threw it over his head and charged through the front door. Inside, everything was crackling. The flames were running through holes in the ceiling. He screamed for Mercy but couldn't even hear himself over the roar. A huge burning ceiling joist blocked the hall, so he ducked into the living room. The smoke was everywhere. He tried to hold his breath but felt himself suffocating. He lost all sense of direction and panicked. His pants and sneakers were on fire. There was no way he was making it out alive.

Somehow, he moved deeper into the house. He tripped over the couch, and Mercy was lying there. There was a bay window above the couch. Cord grabbed a lamp—the metal scalding his palm—and hurled it through the glass. The air fanned the fire, made it worse. He couldn't breathe, but he managed to drag Mercy to the window and pull him through.

Cord remembered the note that fell out of his pocket onto the grass.

Outside, a fire truck pulled in, and someone handed him an oxygen mask. A paramedic performed CPR on Mercy, pushing on his chest and breathing into his mouth until he was finally conscious. Later, the news came down that Mercy's dad was upstairs. The thing he remembered about Mr. Mercy was that he always wore a bucket hat skewered by fishing hooks. He had one ear pierced, and he used to stick fishing lures through the lobe. In the paper it said he fell asleep with a lit cigarette in bed.

Cord wore corduroys that night. It'd been his habit.

As it turned out, corduroys were one of the most flammable materials on the planet, something to do with the fibers. The pants were burned right off his body. There was a scrap of material still covering his ass, but for the most part, he was standing there in tattered underwear in front of fire trucks and policeman and a news crew. The headline in the paper the next day: *Corduroy Kid Delivers Mercy from Fire.*

⁊᚛⁊

Up ahead, a road sign. *Welcome to Bearkill.* It was a small town off the Taconic, named for the black bears that used to wander down from the wooded hills and find their way into people's homes. Bearkill was once home to a thriving mixed martial arts community. It was the town where he and Mercy had started fighting. When his father died, Mercy went to live in a teenage group home, Hillside Home for Wayward Boys, the same quasi-boarding house in Bearkill where Mark had lived for a year. At sixteen, Mercy shared a small room with two other boys. One of the kids there trained martial arts at a small gym with a nondescript name: Chinese Gung-Fu. CGF was in a strip mall next to a biker bar and a jack-of-all-vices shop offering guns, ammo, and tattoos. Mercy took a trial class and was hooked; soon after, he brought Cord out for a look.

Their instructor, Sifu Lao, was a fifty-five-year-old South Vietnamese who'd lost his entire family in the war. Lao had studied Jeet Kune Do under Ted Wong, a first-generation Bruce Lee disciple. Lao taught Wong's non-classical form and added a few "core principles" of his own: good students trained until they puked, toughened their abs with bamboo sticks, struck bare-knuckle until they bled. CGF was a dungeon—a fifteen-foot-by-thirty-foot hole-in-the-wall with a cracked tile floor—no mats—cracked mirrors, and shoddy equipment. Once there'd been a wooden Wing Chun dummy, but the pegs had broken off long ago, turning it into a simple wooden post that students kicked to toughen their shins. There also used to be a heavy bag, but Lao had busted that with a spinning hook kick. Bits of fabric and foam spilled out through the ripped leather.

Cord had arrived at the gym at one hundred eighty-five pounds. After two months, he was a shredded one hundred sixty, a greasy-fast cardio machine. Lao believed in full contact. It was the constant sparring, the *warring*, that turned them into gladiators. One student shattered his knee in three places on the hard tile—and returned three months later with two pins, one titanium rod, and one se-rious *attitude*. The place closed down once Lao moved back to Saigon a few years back, and no two people were sorrier to see it go than Cord and Mercy.

Cord parked and cracked a can of Busch, put the rest on the Celica's hood, and surveyed the parking lot. The biker bar was still there. *GRUDGE*, the sign proclaimed, and underneath: *BIKES-BEER-BABES since 1976, Nifty Mott—Proprietor*.

CGF's space was still vacant, as was the guns-and-ammo shop—a darkened window scraped with grime and dirt. A faded sign hung over the glass: *Coming Soon: Harriett's Arts and Crafts*. From the look of things, Harriett had taken one look at her would-be neighbors and decided to open shop across town.

The bar was pretty much as Cord remembered it: Harleys parked on the curb, choking off the entrance. To go inside you had to navigate a maze of handlebars and shiny chrome exhaust pipes.

A few bikers stood outside puffing on cigarettes beneath a half-lit Budweiser sign, wearing sleeveless leather jackets with snake-eater patches—skull-and-bones with a green tail slithering from the mouth—braided beards, and sunglasses perched over doo-rags with Confederate flag emblems.

Cord was glad to see that CGF had been left unoccupied. It would've saddened him to see the place gentrified—a nail salon or tax office. He was surprised when the knob turned in his hand, even more surprised when he flipped the light switch and the overhead florescent tubes flickered to life, coating the studio with a dirty yellow light. Who was paying for the electricity? Even now, years later, it still smelled like sweat and gym socks. He passed the "changing area," little more than a few fold-up chairs propped against the wall. The bathroom had a single stall. A thick layer of dust blanketed the tiled floor where they used to square off and spar like pit bulls, barefoot and shirtless. You couldn't enter a convenience store like that, but you could sure bash someone's skull.

Lao loved to pit buddy-against-buddy. When he set Mercy and Cord against each other, Cord figured they'd take it easy, throw a few jabs, a few feints, some light leg kicks. But Mercy pounded the snot out of him. Then he raised his arms and hyena-grinned as Cord lay on the floor, dripping blood from his nose and mouth. "Next fighters!" roared Lao. A few minutes later, he came over and dropped an icepack in Cord's lap and said, "You. Next time, fight better."

The next time, he did what Lao said—he fought better—and caught Mercy with a shovel punch to the throat that staggered him. As Mercy held his neck, Cord landed a flying knee to the gut that sent Mercy crashing into the lockers. Lao threw an arm around Cord's shoulders and said, "See? Not mad, *even.*"

Now, Cord ambled to the rear of the studio where a rusted set of lockers hung open. He peered into a few, finding cobwebs and spiders that skittered out of sight. Next to the lockers, the broken Wing Chun dummy rested against the wall like a wooden sentinel that'd performed its last watch duty some years back. He shoved the dummy aside and saw, tucked in the corner, a pair of fighting gloves. He picked them up, ran a hand over the worn leather, and shook off the dust. The label on one glove read, *Title*, the other, *Century*.

He couldn't believe it. Still there, after all these years. The last time he and Mercy had come to CGF, a week after Lao had shipped out, Mercy had said, "Let's leave something behind."

"I already have—my DNA. It's all over that floor."

"As a show of respect, for Lao."

Cord nodded. "Let's each leave a glove."

Mercy agreed. "Mine are shot to shit anyway."

They each tossed a glove in the corner. Then Cord held his remaining glove out to Mercy. "Let's trade." Later, Cord would wonder why he did it, but it had felt natural in the moment. They clasped hands and gave each other a hug that would've made Senator proud then went outside to the parking lot, hearing the door shut behind them for the last time.

"Don't worry," Mercy said. "We'll pick up somewhere else."

"How about someplace with a locker room? Maybe even a working toilet?" Cord tried a laugh that felt strained, even to his own ears. He supposed both knew by then that it wouldn't be the same without Lao.

Now, Cord slipped the gloves onto his hands. They'd each left the opposite-hand glove: Cord left, Mercy right. He tried them out on the air, testing his footwork, his sneakers leaving marks in the dust. His hands found instinctive shadowboxing patterns—jab, jab, uppercut, hook, backfist, hook. He closed his eyes and relaxed into the motion, pulse quickening, sweat beading on his skin, hands curving through open space, as if they were performing surgery on the air. This is how he would remember Mercy. This. Not standing in the cemetery surrounded by hateful strangers.

When he was sweating and out of breath, he staked out a spot in the corner and rested on the floor against the wall. He brought his knees to his chest and bowed his head. He was never one for meditation, but if there was anywhere he could spiritually connect with Mercy, it would be here. With his pulse slowing, a chill worked its way over his skin. He tried to summon his consultation with Celeste, that feeling of weightlessness, like floating through space. He closed his eyes and recited the only type of "prayer" he knew, this time Tennyson's *Ulysses*:

> *Come, my friends,*
> *'Tis not too late to seek a newer world.*
> *To sail beyond the sunset, and the baths*
> *Of all the western stars, until I die.*

He thought of Liana...

∽∾∽

In the days before she cheated on him with Mercy, she had seemed cold and withdrawn. She'd locked herself in her apartment for days. She wouldn't answer the phone. He couldn't concentrate on anything else, hadn't even called to check in with Mercy for more than a week, a rarity for them to go so long without talking. So on Monday morning, Mercy's day off, Cord went over to his place with a twelve-pack.

Mercy answered the door, his trademark grin absent from his lips. He normally wore tight muscle shirts, but that morning he wore an oversized dress shirt—unevenly buttoned and lopsided—the material hanging loosely off his frame.

They sat on the couch, Cord cracking the first beer, guzzling it down in a few long swallows.

Mercy made no move to touch the can Cord placed in front of him. Cord would later remember the way the can perspired, the silent beads of condensation rolling down to form a watery-ring where the tin met the surface of the table—it was the last thing he noticed before Mercy said, "Liana came over the other night."

"Yeah?" Cord felt jealousy twist inside his gut. She'd needed someone to talk to, but she'd chosen Mercy.

Mercy shook his head, stared at the floor. "I was drunk. I hardly remember it, it's all hazy. But I think something happened."

"Like what?"

"Like in bed."

The can of beer slipped from Cord's hand. "You're telling me this now?" All the air in the room seemed to have been sucked out, making it hard to breathe. His pulse hammered at his temples.

"I'm sorry it happened. I feel terrible about it. I can't sleep."

Cord's vision swam. He suddenly felt tired, like he could curl up and go to sleep right there on the rug.

Mercy said, "Say something."

"I can't even fucking breathe."

"Punch me then. Here," he said, standing, "take a free shot."

He shoved his chin forward, but Cord made no move. With blank detachment he saw that Mercy was crying. In a flash, he knew what it felt like to be Barbara—to be numb, to be dead. Rising, he edged around the couch, wandered down the hall, shoved through the screen door and out into the cooling rain. The skies had unzipped, were pissing all over everything. Somehow, he found his way home.

Later, Mercy called. For Cord to accept his apology would mean admitting something *had* really happened, a fact that Cord wasn't ready to confront. He could stand to lose Liana *or* Mercy, but not both, not at once. It was easier to deny it, to distance himself from them both until he could wrap his head around what had happened.

After a while, he and Mercy started training again, like always, but they never mentioned Liana...

∽∾∽

Now, he wished Mercy was alive so he could take him up on his offer—knock the teeth out of his mouth. There were things you didn't do—fuck your best friend's girl, for one. Now he saw the truth: the last two years, he and Mercy had not been the same. They'd talked, hung out, attended each other's fights, but they'd just gone through the motions.

He imagined Mercy's calloused hands on Liana's body, reaching for her hips. A low growl forced its way out of Cord's throat. He launched a sidekick at the wall, put his foot through the rotted particle board. He pulled his sneaker free and readied for another blow when he heard movement behind him. He turned.

He was ready for a fight, expecting the Coroner. Instead, there were two bikers.

One wore a Viking helmet with two curved horns growing from the metal and a tattoo on his bicep, a flaming devil riding a Harley. "Look what we got here," he said. "A basehead on a tweak mission, fighting the wall!"

He laughed and turned toward his partner—cue-ball bald, shorter, wearing enough leather and chains to supply an S & M club, a *Grudge* T-shirt on under his leather jacket—and took a bag of white powder out of his jacket.

"You ain't supposed to be in here," Baldy said. "So beat it, bitch, before we beat your ass."

Cord realized who'd been paying the electricity. If he hadn't been so fired up, he might've walked. With bikers, you had to assume there was a knife, maybe a gun or some sort of exotic homemade getup. It was best to err on the side of caution. But he wasn't feeling cautious at the moment. "What did you call me, you bald fuck?"

Baldy slowly took off his jacket and put down the coke bag. The big man stepped forward with a grin, revealing a row of missing front teeth. "I'm not gonna lie. I was hoping you'd mouth off. It's been a long time since I sent someone to the hospital. Too long."

"I already had my annual check-up," Cord said, already moving forward.

Time slowed as he let his mind go blank, every movement pared down to instinct—the thousands of hours sparring in the gym, the amateur bouts, the mental and physical toil. He was already inside his opponents' heads, anticipating their moves. When the big guy reared back and took a wide-arc swing, Cord easily ducked and exploded upward with an uppercut to the man's gut. The big man's cheeks expanded comically, and he let out a gush of air, doubling over, horns sticking out like a bull ready to charge.

Cord grabbed the horns, yanked downward, and brought his knee up into the man's face. He felt the crunch of teeth breaking on his knee, the jaw snapping sideways. The big man slackened and went down.

Baldy was quicker, sliding behind Cord and throwing a chain over his neck. Cord felt his windpipe being crushed under the pressure, but he had learned long ago to go with the force, which he did, propelling himself and Baldy backward against the wall. He thudded an elbow into Baldy's gut, which made him loosen his grip on the chain. Cord slipped out and turned toward the biker, who squared off like an old-school boxer—a mistake—leaving his midsection and crotch unprotected. Cord launched a front-kick to his groin, and Baldy's knees bowed inward, like a dancer leading the funky chicken. Then his hands flew down to his vitals, a look of extreme concentration fixed on his face, a low moan escaping his lips. He sank to his knees then toppled slowly forward.

Cord swiveled, in case the other biker had regained his feet, but judging from the blood pooling onto the tile, Cord didn't think he'd be standing anytime soon. Cord hauled in a few deep breaths. He felt great. But a feeling of incompletion soon stole over him. His eyes lit on the coke bag, and he snatched it from the floor. On a whim, he dumped the contents onto Baldy's dome. Then he then brushed off his hands and, whistling, strolled out the door.

CHAPTER 15

It was dark by the time he got back to the house. He ran upstairs to change out of his sweaty clothes and found Senator in his room, rifling through his underwear drawer. "Dude, what are you doing?"

Senator jumped like he'd been goosed. In his hands were random items: a sock, a wife-beater, a folded note, blackened at the edges as if partially burned.

Cord's heart lurched when he saw the piece of paper. "Gimme that," he said, grabbing for the paper and stuffing it back in the drawer. "Mind telling me what you're doing?"

"Lovie sent me up here for the bong."

"The bong?"

"He said you had it."

"In my underwear drawer?"

Senator shrugged, peered at Cord from under half-lowered eyelids.

"Looks like you've already had a few hits."

"A few," Senator agreed.

"Get the hell outta here," Cord said, pointing to the door.

∽∾∽

Downstairs, Cord heard a voice call out from the living room, "Cord, is that you?"

Brandi was lounging on the couch in her *Hooters* uniform, her bare feet up on the coffee table, T-shirt clinging to her breasts, short-shorts, flesh-colored tights barely disguising the white trailing scars on her legs—the price of falling off the back of a motorcycle in college.

Lovie sat beside her, a pirate's tricorn feathered hat perched on his head. "Goes with the eye patch, no?" he quipped. He clutched a wooden pipe in one hand, lazy trails of smoke curving through the air. Leonidas was curled up in a fluffy-orange ball beside him. "Straight Durban Poison," he said, offering the pipe. "You're gonna want a hit of this."

"Did you send Senator upstairs for the bong?"

Lovie screwed his face up in a look of intense concentration. "Do we own a bong?"

"Forget it," Cord said. "Shouldn't you be in bed?"

"That's what I told him," Senator said, coming out of the kitchen with a margarita, a lime impaled on the edge.

"And you," Cord said. "This morning you were a wreck. I had to console you for hours. Now you're fine?"

Senator waved him off. "I got over it."

"I showed him my eye," Lovie said with a grin. "That put things into perspective for him."

"It certainly did," agreed Senator.

Cord reached over the coffee table and gave Brandi a hug. She tilted her head back for a kiss. This close, she smelled like a barroom floor—stale cigarettes, spilled beer. "I feel so bad about what happened," she said. "I called you. Why didn't you call me back?"

"Sorry, babe." Cord said, drawing a quizzical look. It hadn't occurred to him to call her back. "It's been a rough couple of days. I didn't want to worry you."

Brandi lived in an apartment on Rotterdam. She'd graduated a year behind the three of them at Pace. After working for two years as an elementary school teacher, she realized she didn't really like kids all that much. Brats, she called them. Ankle biters. So she switched careers and became a Hooters waitress, tripling her take-home pay overnight. Cord had been half in love with her the last year. Or maybe one-quarter in love with her. He loved her breasts, her legs, her violet eyes. But not her nasally voice. Not the smoking thing, nor her habit of flirting with every "gentleman" who came into the "restaurant," as she referred to her workplace and its clientele. And he'd tired of explaining who Nietzsche was, who Wittgenstein was, who—well, all the German philosophers. But she never seemed to mind that their relationship hadn't progressed past the collegiate stage—beer, sex, and more beer—and neither did he.

"I've been pulling double shifts at the restaurant the last three days."

To Cord, it was always comical when she called *Hooters* a "restaurant." There were places that served food and places that featured tits and asses. When they were mixed, traditional designations didn't apply.

"Did you see Cord's new tattoo?" said Lovie, shaking his head. "Morbid motherfucker."

"Let me see," Brandi purred. "I *love* tattoos."

"It's nothing," Cord said.

"Come on, honey."

"Don't call me *honey*. That's what you call your customers."

"So?"

"So why don't you go over to Smiles and start stripping for real?"

"I'd pay to see that," Lovie said, his uncovered eye half-shut.

"Why are you being such an asshole, Cord?"

"Okay, you two," Senator said. "Hug it out."

The doorbell rang, and Senator got up. Cord and Brandi glared at one another for a moment, and then Lovie handed her the pipe. She puffed then lounged into a dreamy doze on the couch.

"Why are we always arguing?" she asked.

"No reason." This was pretty much how things went between them: a nihilistic argument, a drug or alcohol-induced stupor, indifference, sex, oblivion. The perfect girlfriend for his fucked-up life.

"Cord," Senator called up. "There's someone here to see you."

Cord wondered who it was this time. Maybe a few of

Mercy's old buddies from juvie—the self-injurers who liked to carve crosses into their arms and throw themselves through panes of glass—come to claim their pound of flesh.

"Well, look what the cat dragged in," Brandi said.

Leonidas looked up and bared his fangs in a yawn. The summer scent of lilacs crept into the room.

Cord knew, even before he turned, who was standing behind him.

CHAPTER 16

"Bad time?" said Liana.

Lovie's head popped up, like a mole in that game, about to get whacked.

"Don't I know you from somewhere?" Brandi asked, posturing up on the couch, looking conscious for the first time all night.

"This," Cord said, "is Liana. Liana, Brandi."

"I've seen you at the restaurant."

"*Hooters*?" asked Cord.

"They make awesome burgers," explained Liana.

Brandi's eyes searched the ceiling. "*Lee*-ana. Why does that name sound familiar? Oh, *I remember*. You're the bitch."

"Bitch?"

"I've got margaritas, if anyone—" Senator said.

"You know," Brandi said, "I had to listen to him whine for months after you dumped him."

"Did you squeeze in the therapy between lap dances?"

Brandi stood. "At least I didn't fuck his best friend behind his back."

"What did you say?"

Lovie stepped between the two women. "Please, ladies. This is a respectable abode."

"I need to speak with you for a minute, Cord," said Liana. "In private."

"Whatever you've got to say to him, you can say in front of me," Brandi said.

Cord put a hand on Liana's back to lead her away. "We'll be back."

"Corduroy, if you walk off with her, I swear—"

"Chill, Brandi."

இஇஇ

Cord closed his bedroom door behind them.

"Is that your girlfriend? A stripper?"

He shrugged. "She has her good points. I just can't recall them at the moment."

Outside, feet stomped down the stairs, the front door slamming. A moment later came the sound of tires peeling out in the driveway, the smash of trashcans. "She's not much of a driver," Liana said, peering out the window.

"Listen, Liana. You got no right to make fun of her." The temperature in the room seemed to swell as his anger flared again. He found it welcome company. "I went to the gym today where Mercy and I used to train. I had some time to think, and I came to some conclusions. One, I'm pissed that I chummed around with Mercy for two years after what you did—"

"What *I* did? Let's talk about—"

Cord held up a hand. "Let me finish. I should have punched him in the face. *Then* maybe I could've gone to the funeral today and grieved like everyone else."

She crossed her arms over her chest and stared at him.

He let the silence linger. "Two, I spent the past two years pining over you when I should've been cursing you. Instead of writing love poems, I should've been forgetting you. I wanted to be with you. You flushed all that down the toilet, and why?"

"You're not making any sense."

"I came by with flowers and a fucking poem and a wedding ring, and you threw me out. Now that's pretty pathetic, huh?" He breathed heavily, his pulse a series of crashing detonations in his temples.

"And what about *you*?" said Liana. "You and your big mouth. Did you think I wouldn't find out that you told everyone about my stepfather?"

"I don't know what you're talking about."

"Don't lie. You told everyone what he did to those girls."

"I don't know what you're—"

She threw open the door, headed down the stairs, through the kitchen, out the back door. There she whirled and said, "Mark told me everything."

At the mention of his brother's name, Cord felt his insides twist. "What does he have to do with—"

"Like you don't know."

"Liana, listen to me. Mark's up to something. I don't know what."

"I don't believe you," she said. "Trying to pass it off on your own brother."

"Just tell me what happened."

"The week before you and I broke up, I ran into him at the grocery store. He said he'd been praying for me, for what my stepfather did—"

Cord felt like he was stepping late into class, having missed half the lesson. "Wait, what did your stepfather do?"

"He abused my half-sisters." Liana's eyes met his, narrowing to slivers. "There were only five people in the world who knew: my mother and me, *him,* and my half-sisters. And they only knew because it happened to them."

"My God," he whispered.

"Mark said you told him. Do you know how that feels? *You*, of all people?"

"Li, that's a lie. How could I have known? You never told me."

"He said you saw it in my diary."

"I'd never go through your diary." Cord turned and pounded his fist into his palm. How far back did Mark's betrayal go? "The bastard," he said.

Her complexion looked waxen in the porch-lit glare. "You mean you really didn't tell him?"

"Of course not. I didn't know."

"It doesn't make any sense. Why would your brother—" Her eyes widened, and she screamed—a shrill cry piercing the silence—and pointed to the edge of the yard.

He turned, his tattoo throbbing.

It was the Coroner, emerging from the line of oak trees.

"Don't look," he hissed, putting his hands in front of her face. "Just run."

They raced around the porch to the side of the house. When she stumbled, he looked back, saw the Coroner gaining. He didn't seem to be in a rush, moving with a lumbering gait, a malevolent grin sewn onto his face, but every step he took was good for three or four of theirs.

"Faster," Cord yelled, tugging Liana behind him.

He made a move to cut across the lawn, but the Coroner had somehow gotten in front of them. "The car!" Cord screamed.

This time, the giant moved quickly—like he had the second time Cord had seen him, the night at the cemetery. He was going to catch them before they reached the Celica.

"You get in," yelled Cord, shoving Liana toward the driveway, moving to intercept the giant. He lowered his shoulder and collided with the Coroner's chest at full speed. The impact felt like running headfirst into a stone wall. There was no give, only the sickening crunch as his shoulder snapped out of joint. He fell, and the Coroner loomed over him, his cataract eye scanning like a robotic drone. The black obsidian darkness of the other eye stared without purpose. Looking into that eye, Cord felt something—the touch of fingers probing his brain. The same way he'd felt in his dream, lying on a wedge of cold steel, unable to move, the knowledge that he'd died and the Coroner had come to perform his autopsy.

"Cord!"

Her voice delivered him from darkness. The tattoo felt like a searing brand on his neck. The Coroner reached for his throat, but Cord rolled to the side and scrambled to his feet. The Coroner grunted and threw a ponderous hook that Cord ducked. From the car, Liana screamed his name. He darted to the car and hurled himself inside, slamming the door with his good arm. "Go!"

"The keys, Cord. Where are the fucking keys?"

Next to him, a few inches away, the Coroner smashed into his door, and the car rocked.

"The keys!" Liana repeated, as the giant reached back and brought his elbow down, spidering the glass.

"Visor," he said.

Liana dropped the visor and snatched the spare key then jammed it into the ignition slot. At that moment, the Coroner punched through the glass and grabbed for his shirt.

As the tires squealed on the asphalt, Cord heard the fabric of his sleeve coming off in the giant's hands, and the car hurtled backward, out of the driveway.

Liana threw it into drive and hit the gas as the Coroner plodded into the street in front of them. She accelerated toward the Coroner, who stood grinning at them.

Cord braced for impact—but there was only the sensation of parting a fine mist, and nothing else. Just the open road stretching out before them.

CHAPTER 17

My shoulder's dislocated," he said after they'd covered a few miles.

"I'm taking you to Brookhaven."

He shook his head. Something told him if he checked into a hospital—if he stayed in one place, trapped in one room—he'd be dead. The Coroner would get him. He had to keep moving.

"Cord, you're bleeding. Look at the side of your face."

"I can't right now." The pain from his shoulder came in waves, but he was able to fight it off. He'd been in this position before. During his fifth amateur bout, he'd gone for a double-leg takedown, and his shoulder had snapped out of joint. His first loss.

After the fight, his trainer had popped it back into place for him. He didn't go to the hospital then, and he certainly wasn't going to now. "Your mother's a nurse," he said. "Don't you know how to fix a dislocated shoulder?"

She frowned.

"Pull over."

"But what if that monster—"

"He's not following," Cord said. "He's done, for now." He knew somehow that he was safe for the time being. He had a theory: every time the Coroner appeared and vanished, it took him some time to come back, as if he'd used up his strength and had to go somewhere and recharge. That meant they wouldn't see him for a short time. "Stop the car."

Liana pulled into the weedy expanse of a derelict Ames lot. Broken beer bottles clustered around the rusty skeleton of a junked El Dorado, the only feature in the barren landscape. Cord opened the door and stumbled out. The pair of fighting gloves he'd gotten from CGF spilled to the ground. He sat on the gritty asphalt. Liana leaned over him, touching his arm gently. "Quickly," he hissed.

"What if I hurt you?"

"Don't worry about that."

"I'm not really sure—"

"Listen, all you need to do is count to three. On three, yell 'Tom Collins' and pull back as hard as you can. Okay?"

She nodded. He steadied himself against the ground as she rotated his forearm—first toward his body, then away. On the second revolution, she counted, "One, two, three...*Tom Collins*!"

She pulled, he jerked backward, and his shoulder fell back in place with a bone-on-bone snap. He clenched his teeth against the pain, clutching his arm. After a moment, he sat up, rotating his shoulder. It was amazing how quickly the pain fled.

"Nicely done," he said.

"Cord, that tattoo on your neck—"

He resisted the urge to reach back and touch it. "I'll tell you, but not here."

"What about those cuts?"

The lacerations on his arm were long but not deep. "I don't think they need stitches." There was a good gash on his temple, and blood was flowing from somewhere in his scalp, but he was lucky. He could've been blinded, or worse, which made him think of Lovie. "Liana, come here. Let me see your eyes." Her pupils showed no damage, no milky cataract, no Chinese lettering. "Can you see?"

She blinked. "Fine. Why?"

He told her what had happened to Lovie when he'd encountered the Coroner.

"I thought he was just clowning with that eye patch."

In the old days, when Liana would come to the house in costume for her roles, Lovie would likewise play the part. Garbed as Shakespeare's most famous cross-dressers—Rosalind, Julia, Viola—he'd perform with her without knowing the words. After Mindy Shepherd, Liana set him up with her friends, but most refused to see him after the first date. Lovie didn't make a good first-impression—a shame, because he sort of grew on you.

"Did you look at him?"

"Only for a second."

"Maybe that's why you didn't go blind," he said. "Although I've seen him a bunch of times, and I'm fine." *Maybe that's because I'm going to be dead soon*, he thought. *The dead don't need to see.*

"Who is he, Cord? *What* is he?"

"You recognized him? I saw it in your eyes."

She shook her head. "Maybe. I…"

"Tell me."

She gazed down the street, as if expecting to see the Coroner emerge out of the gloom at any moment. "At least let's get you a first-aid kit."

"We shouldn't go back to the house yet."

"We'll go to my place. I've got rubbing alcohol and the drinking kind. I'm sure you could use both."

Cord picked up the fighting gloves, tossed them back inside, and slid into the passenger seat. "You drive."

Liana took him to an apartment complex by the Hudson. When they opened the door, a robed figure strolled down the hall and out of sight. "Who was that?"

"That was Keoni. You remember her, right?"

"That was Keoni?"

"In her Tibetan robe."

"Seriously?"

"You haven't seen her since her transformation."

Keoni was the only one of Liana's friends he hadn't liked. Like Josée, she'd always harbored a grudge against him.

She'd once drunkenly come on to Cord—in a big

way—and he'd turned her down. Back then, she'd dyed her hair a different color every week—fire-engine red, neon purple, banana yellow—and painted her fingers and toenails to match. She'd listened to My Chemical Romance, raved on Ecstasy, and bragged about her clit ring.

"The last time I saw her, she was in County for that bar assault."

"She had a vision," explained Liana. "The next day she took out all her piercings and joined a Buddhist monastery. She just got accepted to the Shang Shung Institute in Massachusetts."

Liana went to find bandages and gauze, leaving Cord to have a look around. The living room had been sectioned off according to the four elements: Fire, Wind, Water, Earth. Flames danced in the fireplace. It felt like a blast furnace in the room's tight quarters, causing him to break out in a sweat. A huge circular fan blew in the Wind section, with crepe paper streamers pulled taut and swimming out from the metal casing. There was a thirty-gallon fish tank in the Water section, harboring no fish that Cord could see. The Earth section was a clumpy mess of dirt and sod. Cord was well accustomed to that look and smell—the open ground of a freshly dug grave. Gashed earth, broken hope.

Keoni wandered into the room wearing a maroon sheepskin robe and sash tie-belt with yin-yang symbols and flower emblems embossed on the fabric. She had a rounded face with slightly slanted eyes, unmistakably Hawaiian.

Her expression seemed vacant. Another corpsestarer, Cord thought. Like Mark. "Hello, Dean." Still not looking at him.

"You've changed, Keoni."

"Keikilani," she corrected. "In this house we are all named after the Gods."

Cord nodded. "I like what you've done with the place."

"This is my inner sanctum. I am at peace here."

"You keep the fire always going, even in the summer?"

"The fire burns eternal."

The silence dragged out. To make conversation, he said, "So, did you end up doing time for that assault on the bartender?"

"The actions of that person no longer concern me."

"What about the girl whose face you smashed in? And the cop you kneed in the balls? I bet they're still concerned."

Liana appeared, carrying a first-aid kit. "You remember Cord, right Kei?"

"His spirit is diseased."

Liana frowned. "That's not a very nice thing to say."

"Can you not see? There's a black mark on his neck, a shadow obscuring his *lhag-mthong*."

"My what?"

"He has no clear path to the *lha-yul*."

Cord nodded. "I know what she means."

Keoni drifted down the hall.

Liana cleaned his wounds and dressed them in gauze. "She's a lot easier to get along with now. If we have a disagreement, she'll just go meditate in her room."

"There are earthworms in that pile of dirt," he said, watching them wriggle.

Liana sighed. "Luckily, I'm not home very often."

"No? Where do you go?"

"The theater, mostly."

She handed him a T-shirt she'd grabbed from Keoni's room. It had a Buddhist inscription: *The secret of existence is to have no fear.*

"That's ironic," he said, looking up. "I'm about as scared as I've ever been."

She led him to her bedroom and closed the door behind her. New room, familiar wall decorations. The same promo for the musical *Cats*, her Bachelor Degree in Film and Screen Studies from Pace, framed tickets from an opening night performance of *Hamlet* at the Broadhurst Theatre. The bookshelf contained her philosophy texts: Locke's *Human Understanding*, Descartes' *Meditations*, and Nietzsche's *Human, All Too Human*. Cord admired her sense of order: the books and CDs alphabetized, her desk and dresser impeccable. She'd once joked that their kids were going to grow up to be neat freaks and germaphobes. Her orderliness was one reason they'd gotten along so well. He noticed a silver bracelet in her jewelry holder. He picked it up. "I didn't know you kept this."

"I had it fixed."

"Why?"

"We can talk about that later. First, tell me what's going on. I want to know everything."

He frowned, unsure of how much he should tell her.

Maybe he could justify keeping her out of it—if he were the only one in danger. But the Coroner had been after both of them. And Mark had gone out of his way to mention Liana. For her sake, Cord had to trust her at least this far. He turned so she could see the back of his neck. "Take a look. It appeared the morning after Mercy died."

She ran her fingers over it, barely touching the skin. "What do you mean *appeared*?"

"I mean I didn't do it. I don't know how it got there."

She felt along his neck, a caress that'd been her habit over the years. Only the last time she'd done it, she'd just gotten out of the shower and was kneeling naked on the bed next to him.

This image brought a deep longing that edged the border of physical pain. A longing he wasn't aware still existed inside of him.

He started explaining—thinking he'd give her the abridged version—but found himself telling her everything, the words spilling from his mouth. He finished by explaining what he knew of Mark's involvement—his bizarre behavior with the photo album, the sickness, how Mark had mentioned Liana's name.

"But what does Mark have to do with that horrible man?" she said when he was done.

"I haven't pieced that together yet."

"Is Jade involved?"

"I just don't know."

"Jade always hated me, especially after that Cayuga Lake incident."

Cord nodded. During his Senior Week at Pace, Mark

had invited him up to the lake. Mark had just earned his masters and had a job lined up at a New York City firm. He wasn't much of a party guy, but he loved to swim. They'd met up with him and Jade on the beach, Mark with sunscreen lining his nose, only slightly whiter than his skin, Jade bulging out of a black one-piece. They'd met at one of his hypnosis conventions in New York City. At the time she'd been bartending but was forced to resign, pending stalking allegations levied by a male coworker.

When Liana got up for a swim, Cord caught Mark's eyes following the curve of her hips. Cord didn't blame him. He couldn't resist sneaking a look himself. Jade had noticed, though, and shot Mark a daggered glance, her emerald eyes boring into him like drill bits.

That night, Mark drank a six-pack and staggered back to the beach, where Liana had gone for a walk.

"He tried to kiss me, remember?" she said.

"How could I forget?"

"Jade was watching from the balcony."

"Mark never heard the end of it," Cord said. "I'm not convinced Jade ever got over that one."

"So you think the two of them are behind everything?"

"A few days ago, I would've said no. But now I don't even know what to think." He paused. "One thing I've been wondering. How did you recognize the giant?"

She shivered. "A dream. The realest dream I've ever had. I was lying on a slab in the morgue. I couldn't move—"

"And you saw *him* standing over you with a saw, ready to do an autopsy."

She looked up, her eyes widening. "How did you know?"

"When did you have the dream?"

"Over the weekend. Sunday."

"I had the same dream, the same day. After Mercy died."

"You were in the dream, too."

"What was I doing?"

"You were in the corner wearing those martial arts gloves, holding a wooden stick. I think you were trying to wake me, to tell me I wasn't dead. Except I couldn't move."

"Is that why you called me yesterday?"

"Yes. And because of what happened to Vic. How is it possible? How could we both dream of that monster *before* we ever saw him?"

"I'm not sure if he even exists."

"I'm not following."

"Didn't you see him disappear when we tried to run him down?"

"I thought he jumped to the side."

"You saw what you wanted to see," Cord said. "He *evaporated*. I saw it happen once before, with Lovie. Something stopped him—I'm not sure what."

"So what is he, then? Some kind of *ghost*?"

Cord studied her face, gauging her response. "A demon, I think."

"I don't believe in demons."

"Li, you saw that giant. That isn't *human*."

She shook her head. "My head hurts, and I really can't process what you're saying right now. I need some time alone to think."

"I think we should stick together. It's not a good idea right now to be alon—"

"Cord. Please."

He lingered for a moment then got up and left. Screw it, he thought. Bitterness crept into his body and lodged there, the same feeling as when she'd rejected him two years earlier. With her, he couldn't win. Why even try?

Keoni called from the doorway. She swept down the walkway carrying a metal pot. "I know what's happening to you."

"How's that?"

"That's not a normal tattoo on your neck."

"Tell me something I don't know."

"Your aura has been perverted by one of the four demons: the Māra of death."

"That sounds like a heavy metal band."

"It's not a joke," she said. "You must accept the severity of your situation or face the consequences."

"Trust me. I do."

"There are four types of demons: afflictions, illnesses, heavenly demons, and demons of death. Yours is a death demon."

"That sounds about right."

"An impediment on the path to Nirvana."

"It feels a lot more serious than an impediment," he said, massaging his shoulder.

"Once, the demon Māra came to Siddhartha as he sat under the Bodhi tree. The Evil One tried to waylay Siddhartha as he meditated, calling forth his beautiful daughters to seduce him, and failing that, legions of creatures to battle him, and yet Buddha remained untouched."

"Okay, but I'm no Buddha."

"There are ways to defeat these evil beings. You must construct a *mandala*, a circular diagram—four gates and a focal point. You may also employ ritualistic symbols, such as the *dorje* or *drilbu*."

"I don't have those on hand at the moment."

"Scepters and ritual daggers are used to kill demons. But anything of symbolic value can be used as protection. All you have to do is empower the symbols."

"How do I do that?"

Keoni smiled for the first time since he'd seen her. "Be creative. To each his own."

"What else can you tell me?"

She looked skyward. "Find out the demon's name," she said. "Then you'll have power over the creature."

"How do I do that?"

Keoni shrugged. "I've only just attained the fourth Noble Truth, pacifism. I haven't learned much yet about invocation."

On a whim, he went out to the car and brought back one of the fighting gloves. "I think Liana should have this, for protection. If she won't take it, hide it somewhere in her room."

"There is one other thing I can offer you," Keoni said, holding out the pot.

"What am I supposed to do with this?"

"I can check your urine for impurities."

"You want me to piss in this? Now?"

She nodded and turned around.

He stood, contemplating her request. He could use any help he could get.

જ્ઞેજ્ઞ

At home, he found an e-mail in his inbox. The subject: *Fight Like Hell*. He frowned and clicked it open. An image depicted two MMA fighters each connecting punches to the jaw of the other. Instead of a cage, the fighters fought within a raised circle of flames. Beneath it read: *YOU, Dean "Corduroy" Masland, are invited to participate in the First Annual FIGHT LIKE HELL mixed martial arts tournament at the New Jersey Civic Center in Edison, April 15, 2016. Sixteen mixed martial artists. One dream. Winner receives $3,500 and a PRO LICENSE.*

April fifteenth. Pain flared at the back of his neck. A great opportunity, he thought. But he couldn't ignore the coincidence of the dates. Getting into a cage right now topped the list of dumb things he could possibly do. Plus, it didn't give him much advance notice. It was risky to take a fight on short notice, but he was never one to back down.

Upstairs, he dug Mercy's fighting glove out of the drawer—where it'd rested since they traded—laying it on the bed next to the one he'd left at CGF. Reunited for the first time in five years. He searched his closet for Bruce Lee's fighting stick.

He rooted around until he found it and placed it next to the gloves. He waited for something to happen—for the stick to glow with an ambient blue light. But nothing changed. The gear didn't look like something that would ward off a demon.

Keoni was wacky, that much was clear. Still, there might be some truth to what she'd said. When Cord had shouldered the Coroner, it felt like hitting a brick wall. Such a collision should've staggered a normal man— even one of such colossal proportions. But the Coroner was not normal, not even close. When Liana ran him down in the Celica, Cord had been certain the impact would split the car in half. Yet it hadn't. Keoni had told him symbolic possessions were the key to defeating a demon.

What did he have in the car that was symbolically significant? The only thing he could think: the gloves. He had been sitting on them in the front seat. He suspected that had somehow saved them. But how?

Had he done what Keoni had suggested? Had he given the gloves power? Online he looked up the words Keoni had mentioned. He learned that the invoker—in this case, Cord himself—could make the artifacts into the equivalent of a spiritual safe haven by simply performing a rite holding reverential significance. He hadn't performed a rite, but he *had* fought with the gloves; he'd used them to put the bikers to sleep. For him, there wasn't much more reverential than a knockout. He decided to keep the glove and stick close at hand. He hoped Liana would do the same with the glove he'd left her. Maybe they would somehow offer protection.

He crawled under the sheets. It was after midnight. He'd made it through another day. He made sure the gear—fighting stick and gloves—rested on the pillow next to him. Then there was nothing to do but close his eyes.

ONE DAY...

CHAPTER 18

At nine the next morning, he woke feeling better than he had in a few days and with a singular purpose. He had a tournament to win. He dialed *Fight Like Hell* and spoke to a secretary who explained that he could still reserve a slot in the prelims as long as he passed a physical and paid the one-hundred-dollar event fee over the phone. Cord had a credit card and enough cash to cover the gas to get there, but he was worried about the physical. Doctors generally frowned upon broken noses and facial lacerations in their clearance considerations.

Next he called Logan Gears, his trainer and coach since Sifu Lao had high-tailed it back to Saigon. Cord and Mercy had joined Team Knock-Down Drag-Out—KDDO—a local martial arts school headed by Gears, a Brazilian Jiu-Jitsu black belt and Muay Thai practitioner. The school had state-of-the-art equipment, a meticulously-kept gym space, and a grappling area big enough to land a Boeing.

A nice place to train, but it lacked the grit of Pound-for-Pound, the menace of CGF. Cord's record since joining KDDO: two and six. His previous record: twelve and two.

"Masland," Gears said in his gruff voice. A conversational tone for Gears was a shout for almost anyone else. Cord had to hold the phone away from his ear as he listened. "I was wondering if you'd ever call."

"As you know, I've been dealing with a few things."

"You think Conor McGregor takes breaks? You ever see Mighty Mouse Johnson slacking off?"

"How the hell would I know, Gears?"

"Let me tell you something, Jimmy," Gears said, his voice raising a few decibels, if that was possible. Gears always called people "Jimmy" regardless of gender, a habit Cord found particularly irritating. "You can either let a bad fight ruin you or take you to the next level. Your choice."

Gears liked clichéd pep talks almost as much as he liked checking his abs in the mirror.

"If you don't count the last fight, I've had six bad fights in a row," Cord said.

"You need to take those losses personally."

"All I've taken is a beating."

"You're not mentally *prepared*, Jimmy. You're letting your coach down." Gears posted his students' combined record on his website. He even had it on his business cards, updated after every fight, currently at three-hundred-five to forty-two. "You're dragging my numbers into the shitter."

"Is that why you didn't tell me about the *Fight Like Hell* tournament?"

"The what?"

"The tournament in Edison, at the Civic Center."

"Never heard of it."

"They're offering the winner thirty-five hundred dollars and a chance to go pro."

"That's the same place they just had a porno convention. You wanna fight or gawk at tits and ass?"

"Look, it's tomorrow. Can you coach me or not?"

"You wouldn't last two minutes in the cage without me," said Gears.

"Is that a 'yes'?"

စာစာ

Downstairs, Cord found Senator reading the newspaper over a glass of orange juice and a soggy bowl of Froot Loops. "Any news on your dad?"

"He's getting arraigned on Friday," Senator said from behind his newspaper. The headline on Cord's side read "The Fall of Valor." "They're expecting him to make a plea bargain. A trial would be a zoo. Prosecution's asking for twelve years, ten with good behavior. I wouldn't be surprised if he got less. If there's one thing my father's good at, it's deal-making."

"Runs in the family, huh?"

"I just keep picturing him hauling me to the ground

under that bathroom sink. I mean, how embarrassing was that? We're lucky no one snapped a photo." Senator moved the paper aside, stared at Cord's face. "Rough night?"

"Aren't you going to offer me a hug?" Cord said.

"This whole thing with my dad has hardened me."

"Pretty soon you'll be as jaded as Lovie."

Senator didn't look well—his eyes shot through with thin membranes of blood, his complexion ashen. In spite of his appearance, there was a gleam of resolve in the set of his jaw that hadn't been there before. He looked like a man who'd chased down the ghosts of his past and left them in a broken heap on the sidewalk.

"You *do* seem changed."

"One can only hope," Senator said, sipping his orange juice. "I always thought my father was an honorable guy. I could never fill his shoes or win his approval, no matter how many charity functions, rallies, fundraisers—I was never going to match up. My brother Kevin was always his favorite. I was the also-ran."

Kevin shared his father's conservative stance on most issues. Like his father he was tall and fit, almost six foot six. Cord couldn't imagine Senator growing up in the same house with those two juggernauts blundering around like rhinos. It must've been hard not to get trampled.

Senator said, "Now I learn that the person I looked up to my whole life is a first-class creep. You should hear what my mom's been saying about him, all this stuff that's now coming out. I think she's going to be on

Oprah sometime next month. Still, it's liberating."

"How's that?"

"He's always harped on me about self-confidence and initiative. Now I realize I lacked those qualities *because* of him. You try being assertive when you have a three-hundred-pound bear charging at you."

"I know the feeling."

"It was all bullshit. My father pretended his whole life, and look how that turned out. I feel like now I can be myself for the first time."

Cord sat back. "Good for you, Senator."

"I need to ask you a question," Senator said, staring intently. "And I want an honest answer."

"Shoot."

"It's about Celeste. What happened back there?"

"I'm not sure, to be honest. But, now that you mention it, I need to make another appointment."

"Seriously?" he said, his face brightening. "You got something out of it?"

"Something. I'm not exactly certain what. But I think she can save my life. Can you get me another session?"

Senator frowned. "You didn't exactly make a great first impression."

"That's why you need to smooth things over."

"I can try. When?"

"How about now?"

"You mean like this week?"

"I mean like right now."

"She requires—"

"Seriously, Senator, this is life or death."

Senator produced his cell phone and hit "two" on his speed dial—"one" was his mother. In a moment, he had the madame on the line.

Cord smiled. Despite their flaws, his friends would do anything for him.

"Celeste?" Senator said. "It's John. I'm sorry to bother you, but my friend Corduroy needs another consultation." There was a pause as Senator nodded and listened. He held the phone away from his ear for a few moments, waiting her out as her voice crackled through the receiver. Finally, Senator broke in, "I know, I know, Celeste. But listen to me, this is life or death."

Cord studied Senator's face: he'd gotten his color back and then some—red blotches now flared high on his cheekbones. His eyes hardened into a stare Cord had never seen before—the glare of an opponent across the cage before the opening buzzer.

"Listen, Celeste. I've been coming to you twice a week for five years. I've bought your products—your relaxation gels, the healing beads. I've spent hours outside your shop, handing out flyers. I'm asking one favor, one time." He listened, nodded, hung up the phone. Senator turned to him. "Inamorata, half an hour. Please, this time, don't wreck the place."

Cord opened his arms in an enveloping gesture. "C'mere, big boy. I think I'm ready for a hug."

Upstairs, he grabbed the fighting gloves and Bruce Lee's stick and met Senator in the car.

CHAPTER 19

"ere's something you should see," Senator said, tossing a newspaper in his lap. "Local section—3A." As Senator drove, Cord found the article.

Local Man Commits Suicide

Ralph Worth, sixty-two, a retired physical education teacher at Havilland High, was found hanged in his High Falls home late Tuesday night. He had been under investigation for charges of child molestation and sexual battery stemming from a 2007 incident.

Worth's girlfriend, Karen Theodore, arrived home from work to find his body in the bedroom of his High Falls home.

He is survived by his daughters, Beth and Vincia Sénécal. Foul play is not anticipated, but inves-

tigators are looking into any possible causes pend-
ing confirmation by the medical examiners.

"Liana's stepfather," Cord said. "He hanged himself last night."

"He was on my dad's campaign committee roster," Senator said.

Cord leaned back in the seat, watched the woodlands fly by. Those poor girls, he thought. And poor Liana, too. Had she also been one of Worth's victims? The thought of it was sickening, made even worse by Mark's deceit. Mark must have discovered Worth's secret and then planned the encounter with Liana. That meant his half-brother had been plotting against him for two years now, at least.

Senator eyed him. "You're thinking of her, aren't you?"

Cord nodded without removing his gaze from the scenery.

Senator clucked. "You still love her, I know you do."

"So what does that prove? That I'm an idiot?"

"You sound like Lovie after Mindy Shepherd got through with him. Next thing you know, you'll be writing poems."

"Lovie writes poems?"

"You should find a way to reconcile." Senator flipped on a radio station.

The talk-show voice pronounced, "…In this day and age, Brady Valor is the norm, not the exception. We need a complete overhaul—"

"Aren't you being a trifle hyperbolic?" interrupted a second voice, this one a low-pitched baritone. "Except for con artists like Valor, the political system is exactly what our forefathers envisioned when they signed the Declaration of Independence. Don't condemn—"

"If Thomas Jefferson were alive today, he'd be falling all over himself to get to the nearest gun shop to blow his brains out—"

Senator pawed at the dial, silencing the radio.

☙☞☙

Inamorata is having a sale! read the sign out front. *Ten percent off all Tarot Readings and Past-life Regressions. Twenty-five percent off Aura/Chakra Readings and Balancings. A healthy CH'I does not come EA—SY!*

Cord retrieved his fighting gear from the back seat and started toward the door.

"What's with the stick and gloves?" Senator asked. "Doesn't that defeat the purpose of shedding bodily limitations?"

"That's exactly what I'm trying to do. I plan on shedding a gorilla off my back. Come on."

They nudged through the doors into the cool incense and bougainvillea-scented interior. Kelly, behind the desk, gaped at Cord's fighting paraphernalia.

"Never mind," he said.

"Normally, we don't have to frisk people, but in your case, it might be appropriate." She held out her hands. "I'll keep those things up front for you. We can't have you going back there armed, right?"

"He'll hang onto them," Senator said, shoving Cord through the curtains. "They have great spiritual significance."

Celeste was waiting for them at the center table, which Cord still thought of as *the mound*. She beckoned with her loose-fitting white sleeves. Senator moved toward a seat on the perimeter, but Celeste motioned him away. He glanced at Cord, like a mother seeing her child off on the first day of school, then disappeared through the threaded beads hanging in the doorway off to the side.

Alone, Cord laid the fighting gear on the table, careful not to disturb the crystal ball, covered in a satin sheath.

"Mr. Masland," she said, her airy voice seeming to come at him from all directions: Celeste in Dolby surround. "Last time I thought I made it quite clear that you were not to return."

"But you didn't tell me why."

"I don't have to explain myself to you."

"You have the ability to help me, but you won't. The only thing I can think of is you're scared."

"Fear is of no consequence to me."

"Then what?"

"You must understand, Mr. Masland. There are greater things at stake here than the mortal coil."

"But this is *my* mortal coil we're talking about."

"If you were simply asking me to save you from the astral plane, I would gladly do it. Saving you from the Fade is another matter entirely."

"*The Fade?*"

"Heaven and hell are black and white terms. There is no pure good and no pure evil, and accordingly no spiritual manifestation of either. There are, however, places where demons can trap souls and keep them for eternity. The Fade is such a place. You may think of it as a place of spiritual jeopardy."

"What can I do?"

"That's what I'm trying to explain to you. Once a demon has become aware of a person through an earthly medium, the demon's gaze cannot be broken. Once invoked, the demon becomes simpleminded, possessed of a singular purpose."

"You *are* scared. I can smell it. You don't want to put your ass on the line. Am I right?"

Celeste's face wrinkled for a moment then regained that impassive, glazed-over calmness. Cord imagined a younger Celeste, a woman empowered by anger who had found spirituality as the means to protect herself. "Fear is intrusive to my spiritual well-being."

"But there's something you're not telling me."

"In my younger years, I might have helped you out of pride."

"And now?"

"I'm not so foolish anymore."

He moved to pick up his gear, but she stopped him. Her touch was icy cold. "Sit down," she said with a sigh. "And don't ask any more questions."

He did as she instructed.

"Are you a brave man?"

"Yes."

"Are you ready to fight the demon for your life?"

"Yes, dammit."

"You will have one chance. Though it will be a fair fight this time. I sense the empowerment in these gloves and stick. *Use them*. Defeat him."

"Okay." He felt his heart begin to pound as it always did before a fight, and yet once the bell rang in the cage, he always felt as calm as could be.

Celeste closed her eyes and ran her fingers over the stick and gloves—the worn wax wood, the scraped leather. "Close your eyes," she said. "Place your hands over mine. Do not break the grip, no matter what happens."

In a moment, he could feel heat radiating through the center of the table. He realized it was coming from his gear. He had no doubt that if he opened his eyes he would see the gear glowing a hot orange-red, like a piece of newly-forged metal.

"Let us travel."

Her voice seemed to come to him from afar. He expected to experience the same weightlessness as before, but this time the impression was jarring, like dipping down on a rollercoaster. Images rushed at him in a mad jumble: the skies reddening, the grass withering to dust, the trees shrunken and misshapen. He passed through a gate of twisted-black iron, posts rising hundreds of feet in the air, and over a snaking river—Acheron—obsidian waters gashed with swaths of red blood. Cord saw a boat drifting over the waters and its ferryman—vermillion eyes floating inside a black hood—and he knew exactly where he was. But Celeste said there was no heaven or hell, he thought. Then he realized this was *his* interpretation of the Underworld, from what he'd read in literature. He was seeing the hell in his own mind.

Dantesque visions: weeping pagans, born before Christ and unsaved; adulterers fawning over one another, perpetrating the same acts that had condemned them in life; gluttons eating their own filth; wrathful soldiers shoving spears into their opponents' scarred bodies; heretics, prophesying man's downfall.

Cord came upon the great Minotaur—gladiator's body, bovine head, two curved horns shooting skyward. The Minotaur stood aside, and Cord saw an army of centaurs, tawny limbs firing arrows into the bodies of the sinners who died enacting violence against others, and beyond, the suicides. There were winged demons with lion tails, hairy goat demons flying like flocks of ravens.

Then he was standing before the Coroner. The giant was hunched over a stone slab, gouging a corpse with rusty surgical tools, bloody bits of bone spackling his white lab coat. The corpse's mouth was open, entrails tucked to the side. Cord couldn't scream, couldn't turn away.

The Coroner turned toward him suddenly, regarding him with his cataract eye. Cord felt a strange gurgle in his throat and realized he was being forced to speak. When he spoke, it was with Celeste's voice, "I have passed through the gates to travel to your sanctum. I command you now, with the power of one who has traversed the Astral Plane, *tell me your name*."

The demon opened its mouth; gristle stuck in its craggy beard. "I am Sphir."

"Then come, Sphir."

Cord felt a pull from behind, and the images blurred, too fast to recognize. There was a jarring impact as he slammed back into his body. His eyes flew open. Celeste released his hands.

"The demon will not be far behind. Are you ready?"

"*Now?*"

As she nodded, he felt something stir inside, a manic anticipation. He wanted another shot at the Coroner, a chance to end the curse.

"Put on your gloves. Pick up your stick," Celeste said.

He did. They radiated heat. His fingers curled around the smooth wax wood. In his mind he was already using it to bash the Coroner's skull.

"Quickly, he's coming," said Celeste. "I will bring you to a familiar place. Show him no mercy, since he will afford you none."

She put her hands over his eyes, and immediately the cage materialized. The Coroner stood across from him, still wearing the blood-spattered lab coat. Cord looked down at his hands—he wore Mercy's gloves and held Bruce Lee's stick, which glowed a dull amber. An angry murmur ran through the crowd, a spattering of boos. Fuck 'em, he thought. Might as well play the heel. A murderous thrill ran through Cord as he brandished the fighting stick, the wood now burning hot. The Coroner powered forward. Cord swung the stick in a sideways arc and slammed it into the demon's gut. The cataract eye widened in a startled look of pain and surprise. Again, Cord drove the stick into the Coroner's midsection, driving a great bellow of air from his lungs. The demon sank to one knee.

"How's that feel, big guy?" Cord raised the stick again, readying to slam it against the unprotected cervical curve of the demon's neck.

Suddenly the wax wood turned from ocher to red and began to smoke. Cord flung the stick from his burning hand then slammed a hammer-fist down on the demon's neck, dropping him to the floor. As the Coroner raised his head, a worm of blood running down his temple, Cord threw a corkscrew punch that smashed into his forehead then an axe kick to the back of the head. The Coroner collapsed onto his stomach. Cord lunged onto his back, raising the demon's head and slamming it against the canvas—once, twice, three times. Then, as he readied for a finishing blow, the backs of his gloves suddenly caught fire, the *Title* emblems blackening then curling. He whipped off the gloves and tossed them to the mat where they ignited the canvas in flaming circles.

The Coroner picked himself off the canvas, growling like a wounded beast. The demon lunged.

Cord retreated to the far side of the cage and screamed, "Celeste!"

Instantly, he felt the same tug he'd felt in the Seventh Circle and was sucked backward through the cage.

cↄeↄ

His gear lay on the table, an unrecognizable mess of charred leather and wood. The room smelled like a burned compost heap, all traces of the fragrant patchouli gone. Celeste put the back of her hand against her forehead as if testing for a temperature. Her hood was pulled back, her hair matted down, displaying patches of mottled scalp between silver braids. A line of blood trickled down from her nose onto her upper lip.

"Are you okay?" Cord asked, still breathing heavy. A numb detachment settled over him like a shroud, the way he always felt after a fight—and particularly now, when victory had been so close at hand.

Celeste gave him a kind smile that made Cord wish he'd never gotten her involved. "I tried," she said, procuring a handkerchief and dabbing at the trail of blood seeping from her nostril.

"What happened?"

"I don't know," she said. "I sensed an evil force creating the fire that burned your artifacts."

Mark, Cord thought. It had to be him. The curse would be fulfilled—Mark would see to that. Somehow he'd sabotaged their efforts. Cord didn't understand how, but in the end, did it really matter? That bastard was going to pay—in this life or the next.

Suddenly Senator appeared in the beaded doorway, surveyed the scene. "What's that smell?"

"Don't ask," Cord said.

Kelly appeared and helped Celeste to her feet, noticing the blood trickling from her nose. "Get out. Both of you," she said.

Outside, the *Rocky* theme blared. Cord snapped the phone open.

"I'm seeking your salvation, but you won't let me help you."

"Mark?"

"'Their foot shall slide in due time: for the day of their calamity is at hand, and the things that shall come upon them make haste.' That's *Deuteronomy 32:35*."

"I'm coming after you, brother. I just kicked your demon's ass. You're next."

"A demon, my word." Mark brayed laughter. "Did you give Liana my best?"

"Leave her out of this."

"In time, brother. In time."

Cord's mind went blank. All he could manage was, "Wait."

❧❧❧

Cord sat on the curb, his feet hanging out into the street. He listened to the sounds coming from the nearby kennel: yipping barks, deep-throated growls, squeals of delight. A mother marched a group of howling children into the kennel. One of the kids glanced at him, a finger shoved up his nose. The smell of dog shit permeated the air.

"'O, my offence is rank, it smells to heaven,'" Cord said. "'It hath the primal eldest curse upon it, a brother's murder.'"

"Did you write that?" Senator said, appearing beside him.

"You're a drama queen. Haven't you read Shake-speare?"

Senator's face colored, and he pointed at Cord. "Don't take your bullshit out on me. I'm just trying to help."

"I'm sorry, buddy." Cord sat for a moment then dialed Liana's number.

When she picked up, she sounded out of breath. "Cord, something's happened."

"Wait. You have to do something right now. I left a glove with Keoni. Go get it. Don't let it leave your sight."

"The glove—wait, that was yours?"

"Have you seen it?"

"I threw it away," she said. "Garbage pick-up was this morning."

"You what?"

"I found it under my bed. It smelled gross, like old gym socks."

CHAPTER 20

After dropping Senator at the house, Cord raced the backstreets to Liana's apartment. When he got to the door, he was half-convinced the Coroner would answer, holding her limp body. As hell's mortician, the dead *were* his business.

When no one answered, he shouldered open the door. "Anybody here?" Liana's bedroom light was on, the door ajar. "Li?"

He heard the water from the shower. He knocked. "Liana, it's Cord."

The water turned off, the sound of a shower door.

Liana stood in a swirling cloud of steam, towel wrapped in a line across her breasts, dark hair hanging into her face.

"What's wrong?" he asked.

"Look."

She pulled her hair into a ponytail and turned her

back to him. Her bare neck glistened with jewels of moisture.

No, he thought.

Her neck bore an identical tattoo to his. The
birthdates were different, but the death date—April 15,
2016—was all too similar.

"Get dressed," he said. "We're not safe here."

"I don't understand any of this."

"We don't have time to talk right now. We need to
move."

He waited in the hall while she threw on some
clothes. If his theory about the Coroner was right, they
might be safe for an hour or two. When the demon came
back tonight, Cord sensed it would be impossible to stop
him. Cord couldn't buy another pair of fighting gloves,
for the same reason he couldn't replace Bruce Lee's stick.
He had given those items power, had charged them blow-
by-blow. The Coroner had been rocked. He'd retreated to
the cage. But now, without his gear—Cord had nothing.
He couldn't run. Where could he go to escape a demon?

In the golden late afternoon sun, he drove back to his
house with Liana. He feared turning a corner to find the
demon standing in the middle of the road. He glimpsed
things on the periphery—dark, flitting shapes that vanished when he turned to look full on. It sickened him to
see the crisp blue-black edges of the tattoo on Liana's
neck. He wanted to return to the time before—before
he'd killed Mercy, before all this madness began. And
now Liana was involved. The only woman he'd ever
loved—and he was dragging her into the same grave with

him. It didn't make sense that she, too, had been marked. She was innocent in all this. After all, it was *his* goddamn curse.

Neither of them spoke during the car ride, except once—as they passed Woodside Cemetery:

"'The demon waits and waits and will be satisfied,'" said Liana.

Cord recognized the line. "Nietzsche."

ᐸᑐᐸᑐ

Back at the house, Lulu regarded him warily, her triangulated mouth pressed up against the glass, her tail swishing through the water. She hadn't been fed in more than a day. Things were bad when he forgot to feed his fish. He glanced at the mattress: thrown-back covers, rumpled sheets. His life was unraveling like a spool of thread. He was losing himself—one neurosis at a time— forgetting the little things that made him tick.

He made a move toward the fish tank, but Liana beat him to it. "Hey, Lu," she said, bending so her face was level with the glass. "Where's Rocky?"

Cord cleared his throat. "He went belly-up the other day. I buried him out back, away from the cat."

"Lu, you poor thing." She sprinkled dry flakes of fish food into the tank. "You must be lonely."

"She's been eating the other fish."

Liana frowned. "Now that's not nice," she said. "It seems like just yesterday I bought them for you."

"Try six years."

"How long do angelfish live?"

"No idea. But Lu's a survivor. Isn't that right, Lu?"

Lulu snatched at a flake of food that'd descended to her level, her blood-red eyes boring holes in the glass.

Liana sat on the bed, pulling her knees to her chin, a signature pose. Cord sprawled on his back and tucked his arms behind his head. He reached to turn on the stereo. A dilemma: Liana liked classical, but he liked metal, one of the few things they'd argued about during their six years. He took the middle ground and popped in a Trans-Siberian Orchestra CD—sitars, piano, and shredding guitars. "When did the tattoo appear?"

"Today. In the double mirror. I saw it back there. What does it mean, Cord?"

Cord paused. What good would it do, lying to her? "I think it means exactly what it says. We have a day left to live."

She frowned. "This is Mark's curse, isn't it? Why don't we just drive over there and make him take it all back?"

"It's not that easy. He hypnotized me or something. I can't get near him without getting really sick."

"I can. I'll just go over there—"

"By yourself? And do what? Punch him in the face?"

"If I have to, sure."

"And what about Jade?"

"I'll take care of her too, Cord. I'm not as dainty as I look."

"I'm not gonna argue that, but what about their kids?"

"At this point, I'm not so concerned about posterity."

"And if one of them calls the cops on you?"

Liana threw up her arms. "I don't know, okay?" she yelled. "All I know is we have to do something. Something other than sitting here, waiting to die."

"I'll figure something out, okay? Right now, let's go back to the beginning and make some sense of this."

"Starting where?"

"Starting with your depression, two years ago. You locked yourself in your apartment for days. You stopped going to work. Stopped calling me or even answering your phone. Why?"

"Why? Does this have some bearing on our current situation?"

"It might. If we're going to figure this thing out, we'll need all the information we can get."

She stared off into space—as if she were on stage, about to deliver a soliloquy. "I can't tell you."

"Don't give me that bullshit," he said. "Just once, I'd like to hear you come out and say something original, something in your own words. Do you even remember what those sound like?" A ragged smile edged across his lips. "You want to know the difference between you and a normal actress? When the curtain comes down, *you're* still acting. Get over yourself."

He expected tears—her defense against him—but incredibly, she grinned.

"Well, Mr. Masland," she said. "I do believe you've put me in my place."

"First time for everything."

She paused then gathered herself. "You can never say anything about this, not ever."

"I promise."

"It started with my stepfather," she began. "Beth, my half-sister, mentioned that he came into her room at night to read *Charlotte's Web* to her. She said she had a *secret* between her and Ralph. She said he touched her down there with his mouth." She brushed a dark curl out of her face. "The same day, I spoke to my other half-sister, Vincia, who repeated the same story—Ralph coming into their room at night after Mom was asleep. I told Mom, and she kicked him out of the house, and he swallowed a bottle of sleeping pills down at the train station. A cop out, if you ask me. If you want to kill yourself, you don't do it in a public place. At least this time he finally got it right."

Cord stared at Liana, deciding how to ask the question that'd been on his mind ever since hearing about Worth. He had a day left to live and a demon hunting him, and yet the Coroner was about the farthest thing from his mind.

"Li, did Ralph ever—"

"I don't know, Cord," she said, answering his unspoken question. She'd always been able to read his mind. "I really don't."

"How can you not know?"

"It's a blank. I don't remember anything like that happening to me. I have very few early memories of him at all."

Cord let out a breath. "Did you repress it, maybe?"

"How could I know that?"

"Could he have started with the girls?"

She slid her hand into his palm, worked her fingers between his. "I called him," she said. "Yesterday after you left. I told him he should die. I told him I wanted to kill him myself. And you want to know the sick thing? I don't feel bad that he's dead, just a sense of relief."

"Did he deny it?"

She shook her head. "When I was done, he said, 'I'm sorry.' As if that made it better. Then I asked him if he did that to me, too. I screamed at him to tell me. All he said was, 'Goodbye, Liana.' He took his secrets with him to hell."

Cord brushed the hair off her neck, slowly ran his finger along the edges of the tattoo. He felt a shiver pass through her body, but she didn't try to remove his hand. The design was perfect, the black edges crisp. He wondered if it would disappear when the curse was fulfilled. *If* the curse was fulfilled. He had to keep reminding himself they weren't dead yet.

"Why didn't you tell me?" he asked. "I could've been there."

"I had to think about the girls first. No one could know. Not even you."

"Then Mark came along."

"Yes. And I believed him. I'm sorry for not trusting you. It still doesn't explain how he found out in the first place, though."

A part of him wanted her to continue through to the end, to explain her betrayal with Mercy. But he'd had enough revelations for one night. And all this talk wasn't keeping them out of danger.

He thought of his roommates, of the danger he might be bringing down on them. He stood. Lulu's feral eyes charted his every step. "We have to tell Senator."

"You mean to tell me you haven't told your room-mates?"

"No. It seemed too, I don't know—"

"Bizarre?"

Cord nodded. "Even for them. But they need to know. The demon might appear any minute, and if they try to stand in the way—"

"Then they're dead, too."

"Look what already happened to Lovie. I can't have that happen."

"You go. I need to rest. If a demon breaks in through the window, I'll scream, and you can come save me."

"Scream loud."

"Don't worry. I will."

CHAPTER 21

Cord searched the house but found no sign of Senator, although his Volvo was in the driveway. He did find Lovie on the couch asleep, an open bottle of Smirnoff on the coffee table. "Wake up, buddy."

His eyelids struggled open, like a set of broken Venetian blinds. "Cord?"

"Why are you drinking in the afternoon?"

"I needed a stiff one." He struggled to a seated position then jammed his palms against his temples and rubbed. "To even things out."

"Where's Senator?"

"Fuck if I know."

"His car's parked out front."

"Try the basement. I heard someone banging around down there. And, this time, I wasn't going to check."

Cord went down the basement steps and turned toward the furnace room. The door was closed, a flickering light dancing underneath. He nudged open the door.

The first thing he noticed was Senator, crouched in a circle of lit candles, wearing only his boxers, his skin oily-brass in the wavering candlelight. Within the circle, chalk lines ran in a pentagram shape, the number *fifteen* scribbled across the concrete floor. Senator clutched something in one hand, his lips moving soundlessly, eyes closed. Cord recognized the thing in his hand: his fighting glove.

"Senator?" he whispered.

Senator's eyes fluttered open.

"What are you doing?"

Senator glanced down. The glove fell from his grasp. "I wanted to tell you, but I didn't know how."

"Tell me what?"

"About the demon."

Cord grabbed Senator by the shoulders and pinned him against the door, Cord's forearm across his throat.

"Let me explain, Cord." Senator choked out the words.

"You sonofabitch. Tell me."

"I will if you give me a chance to explain."

Cord pulled back. "Talk."

Senator rubbed his throat. "I know what's going on, Cord. I know the trouble you're in. I was trying to help."

"Where'd you get my MMA glove?"

Senator picked up a small brown box on top of the furnace and handed it to Cord. "It came in the mail for you."

"You opened my mail?"

"It was addressed to you, from Vic. I thought you might be too upset to open it. So I did it for you. When I saw what was inside, I thought you could use it as protection, like you did at Inamorata. I'd been searching for something of yours that held spiritual significance. I think I found it."

"Are you saying you know everything—the curse, the demon?"

Senator nodded. "Celeste told me."

"Why didn't you say something?"

"Why didn't you?"

Senator held out the package the glove had come in. The name on the return label read *Vic Mercy, C/O Adrienne*. Vic's aunt, the woman who'd had power of attorney for him as a teenager.

"Let's go upstairs and figure this out," Senator offered.

Cord paused at the door. "Senator, why are you half-naked?"

"It's easier to channel my ch'i without clothes."

"You said it."

ᘓᘎᘓ

After Senator dressed, they went out to the porch and slumped into the patio furniture. "I owe you an apology, buddy," Cord said.

Senator waved him off. "I'll bill you for the crushed trachea."

"It's been a bad week."

Senator shivered despite the warm night. "He's awful."

"The Coroner? You've seen him?"

Senator shook his head. "It's more like I *felt* him, at Inamorata. That's why I decided to try my luck at a few protection spells."

Cord studied his hands. "You remember that reading you did for Liana and me?"

"A couple years back?"

Cord nodded and pointed to his neck. "She's got the same tattoo. April fifteenth. Tomorrow."

Senator gaped at him. "No."

Cord had never paid much attention to palm lines. Before he met Senator, he didn't know his life line from his heart line. When Senator had read their palms that one day, he'd said their life lines intertwined until a point, then diverged. Both of their lines were shallow after that point, barely there. Afterward, Senator had privately shared his opinion: one or the other, Cord or Liana, would continue, not both. Now, with the Coroner after both of them, it looked like divergence had arrived. If sacrifice was required, Cord was going to make sure it was him. "If you were right about that reading—"

"Spiritual readings are things that *might* be," Senator said. "They're more like warning signs."

Cord checked to see if the back door was shut so they wouldn't be overheard. "If you were right, it would mean I might have a chance to save her."

Senator went silent for a long while. "We haven't tried a Tarot reading yet. Are you up for it?"

"Will it help?"

৵৩৵৩

Cord checked on Liana in his bedroom, finding her fast asleep. Then he joined Senator in his room down the hall. The room smelled of incense and hydrangea flowers. Electronic techno/trance filtered through the stereo. Senator spread out a black tablecloth and lit candles in a wide circle.

He fanned Tarot cards in front of him. The deck read simply, *Fate*.

Senator had put on a red velvet robe. He sat cross-legged, muttering to himself with his arms crossed in his lap, palms-up, like a Tibetan monk. Cord slipped into the circle.

After a moment, Senator shuffled the deck of cards and placed them in front of Cord, who cut them at the midway point. Senator then reassembled the deck and fanned them out, sigils pointing down.

"Choose," he said in a baritone voice Cord didn't recognize.

Cord picked a card and handed it to Senator, who turned it face up. The sigil showed a woman kneeling on a beach, azure-blue ocean in the background. She held two swords, crisscrossed over her heart.

"The Two of Swords," Senator said. "Duality. Balance. The swords are stalemated, neither has any advantage. Since the swords are crossed over the heart, it can also mean a closed heart, denying true feelings. It's not necessarily opposition, but a barrier against revealing the truth. The barrier will eventually break."

"And what does that mean?"

"In a relationship sense, it could mean there's a barrier between you and someone. Secrets, say. These barriers must be taken down piece by piece or else they will collapse all at once. Pick again."

Cord drew another card. An eight-spoked wheel superimposed over a backdrop of clouds and sky, crested by a Sphinx adorned with an Egyptian headdress. Four-winged figures were posted at the corners: lion, ox, eagle, man. A horned creature ascended to the right, a snake to the left.

"Wheel of Fortune."

"Meaning?"

"Destiny. Circle of life. It may also mean change."

"How?"

"If you're at the bottom, change would bring you higher. If you're at the top—"

"I don't think I have to worry about that."

"The wheel implies that everyone's lives are connected. In order for someone to ascend, someone else must fall."

"What do the figures represent?"

"These are astrological signs. Leo, Taurus, Scorpio, and Aquarius. The other two are the gods Anubis and Typhon, generally associated with death and destruction. Pick again."

This time, the card depicted a man hanging upside-down from a natural cross made in a tree. He was hanging by one leg, the other crossed behind his knee. There was no fear in the man's face. Instead, he wore an enlightened countenance, a yellow halo surrounding his head. "The Hanged Man," Senator said.

"What does that signify?"

"Sacrifice. He has the nimbus aura of a martyr. He must sacrifice his free will and power in the physical world to regain both in the spiritual plane. Final card. Pick."

Cord picked for the last time. It was a human skeleton wearing chainmail and a helmet with a feathered crest, a black flag with the symbol for poison trepanned through its forehead.

"Death?" asked Cord.

Senator nodded. "Forced sacrifice."

The trance CD ended. In the silence, Cord drew in a ragged breath. The candles and incense choked the air, making it hard to breathe.

Senator moved his lips silently. As Cord watched, his eyes rocked back to the whites like reels on a slot machine.

"Senator?" he whispered. "What's wrong?"

"Three riddles," Senator croaked.

"What are you talking about?"

"What has no beginning and no end—round and round, it bends and bends?"

After a moment's hesitation, Cord grabbed a pen and paper from the desk and scribbled down the words.

"What has ink but never writes, a beak that always bites?"

Cord wrote, and Senator spoke the final riddle.

"What is harvested but not sown, turns from white to roan?"

A few moments later, Senator's eyes flicked back into focus, and he stared at Cord like someone coming to after being kayoed. "What happened?"

"Don't you remember?"

"No."

"You just told me three riddles." Cord held out the paper. "What do they mean?"

"How should I know?" Senator crinkled his brow, staring at the sheet. "The last one's easy. Harvested, not sown. Harvest moon. It's the moon."

Cord nodded. "I know the first. A ring. It has no beginning, no end, and it's round. I think I remember that one from back in grade school. What about the middle one?"

"Beak, like a bird? What kind of bird has ink? A sparrow?"

"Maybe."

They heard voices in the hallway, and Lovie wandered in. "What the hell's gotten into you, Cord? Tarot cards?" Lovie demanded, pronouncing Tarot like *carrot*.

"We're trying to solve a riddle," Senator explained.

Cord shot him a look: *The fuck would you tell him that for?*

"He's good at riddles," Senator said. "What has ink but never writes, a beak that always bites?"

Lovie tilted his head, his face screwed up in a look of consternation.

"You'd have to have a few brain cells left—" Cord said.

Lovie shrugged. "That's easy. An octopus. Got any more?"

CHAPTER 22

For dinner they had beef and mashed potatoes with thick gravy and homemade apple pie, Senator's special recipe. Cord shoved away from the table and picked up Mercy's glove. He ran his hands over the worn leather, the duct tape still holding, even after all these years.

"I don't understand why these gloves are so important," said Liana, stifling a yawn.

Cord told her about the last day at CGF, how he and Mercy had swapped gloves, how he'd later used the gloves as talismans.

"So we should be safe then?" Liana said, taking the glove. "With this?"

"Yes," Cord said, to reassure her. He wasn't all that sure himself. Fighting with one glove—it would be like going to bat with a helmet that only covered half his head. He was bound to take one to the skull.

Cord wanted to discuss the riddles with Senator, but not in front of Liana. He didn't want to worry her any further. "Senator, do you know anything about hypnosis?"

He'd been replaying the scene in his bedroom when Mark had held the homerun photo, twirling it between his fingers. Mark must have hypnotized him, Cord concluded, and planted the idea of sickness in his mind. It explained his physical reaction, but what about the demon? Could he have somehow made Cord hallucinate the encounters? Not possible, because Liana had seen him, too. A demon was a demon. The tattoo was real, a design that Liana now shared. That was no hallucination. "I think Mark hypnotized me. If someone can de-hypnotize me, maybe I can get to him."

"Keoni might know something about that," Liana said.

"Call her."

Liana called but got her voicemail. "She's away on a nature retreat tonight. It'll have to wait till tomorrow."

"Tomorrow may be too late." Cord turned to Senator, "What's the significance of the number fifteen?"

"I can answer that one," Liana said. "April fifteenth. It's our death day. Tomorrow."

"But Senator had it scrawled on the floor."

"No spell can go on indefinitely," Senator said. "All curses and spells have a half-life."

"I'm not following."

"The duration the curse has to take effect. Finding out a curse's half-life is a simple matter of a few incantations and proper astral projection line calibrations."

"How about in English?" Cord said.

"If a curse reaches its maturation point and the half-life ends without completion, it reverts back to the caster."

"It ends after the fifteenth."

Senator nodded. "Tomorrow night. Either you…expire…or the spell reverts to the caster."

A thread of hope buzzed through Cord. If they could stay alive until then—

At that moment, Lovie barged into the room. "That creep is standing outside, just staring at the house."

Cord went to the window looking out onto the front lawn. He pushed aside the curtain, but he already knew who was there. The Coroner stood with his arms crossed at the edge of the lawn. He wore the lab coat, still spattered with blood. He pointed at Cord and made a cutting motion across his throat then stepped back into the woods.

"It's *him*, isn't it?" asked Liana.

"He's gone," Cord said. "For now." He couldn't understand why the demon hadn't attacked. It was like he couldn't come onto the property. Something was keeping him at bay. The glove, Cord thought. Whatever Senator had done to the glove.

"Did you see him?" asked Lovie.

"Listen, Lovie," Cord said. "If you see that guy again, do *not* look at him. Just turn the other way."

"Who is he?" Lovie asked.

"A dead man, if I have my way."

Cord shoved his hand into the fighting glove, meeting with resistance: a folded piece of paper. He pulled it out. When he saw the handwriting, he went into his bedroom and closed the door behind him.

> *April 7, 2016*
> *Cord,*
>
> *Hey, bud. If you're reading this, it means I'm dead. Tough break, huh? When I got sick, I made up a will. I don't have much—you know that—but I wanted to make sure you got this package. You're probably thinking, "Great, his aunt gets the old Chevelle, and I get a ratty old glove." That piece of shit car was on its last legs, anyway. This is way more important.*
>
> *I'm not good at writing, and I hate long-winded letters, so I'll try to keep this quick. I have an aneurysm in my brain. I went to the doctor, and he gave me an MRI and told me to quit fighting immediately. He said I can't fight or do any sports, anymore. It's in a bad spot, and he can't operate. He said it might hemorrhage at any time, no telling when. I waited a long time to go to the doctor (you know me with doctors) after I started getting the headaches, so maybe it's partly my fault. Maybe they could've done something if they'd caught it earlier.*
>
> *You can't imagine what it's like, knowing you can never do the things you love to do. That your time is a lot shorter than you thought. There were*

so many things I never did. Remember that plan we had to fly to Thailand and enter one of those Muay Thai tournaments or the Brazilian World Championships in Sao Paulo? I mean, I never even got to go scuba diving. But the day they first told me, I had all these ideas running around in my head. I didn't know what to do first. I would've probably sat there all day undecided, but then I ran into your brother, and we got to talking about you and how it was growing up. We talked about Sterling Lake, and maybe it was the aneurysm or the shock of the news, but the next thing I knew, I was there at the lake.

It was cold, but in the sun it wasn't so bad. I had the whole lake to myself. You know how on some mornings, the fog can get thick, and you can't even see a quarter of the way across? That day it was so clear I could see all the way to the old boathouse, a couple miles away. The sun was bright, casting this glare across the surface. I thought I could walk across the path it made on the water. I started crying. Can you imagine that? Me, crying out by the lake like that? It seemed important to appreciate every moment. I didn't want to close my eyes, thinking I'd miss something spectacular I'd never see again. It might be the last time I'd visit that lake, see those willow trees, hear the humming of the cicadas.

I dozed off and had this crazy dream. You were in it. And Liana. You and I were in the cage, she was in the audience. I knew it was my last fight, that I was going to die in that cage, but I wasn't scared. When we started fighting, my headache got real bad. I knew if I caught you with a straight, you would throw a right hook, like you always do—only this time I wouldn't block it. It happened in slow motion, your swing connected, and there was an explosion in my head, and my vision on that side went out. I fell to the canvas. I knew I would die. And it felt good, that knowledge. It's how I wanted to go out, in the cage, fighting with my best friend. Much better than wasting away in some hospital. I saw Liana climbing into the cage, throwing her arms around you. Then I realized: with me dead, you two could be together. You two could be happy again, like before I screwed everything up. I felt it in my heart.

Well, so much for being quick. It's the last letter I'll probably ever write, so at least I got my money's worth. Now you know why I never told you about my condition. You can't save me, brother, not this time. And I love you too much to ruin your shot at happiness. You two belong together. I always knew that, and now I can make it right. I hope you're reading this with Liana. I can see her smiling next to you, holding your hand.

—Always, Vic

P.S. I found this glove in my closet. Remember when we switched the last day at CGF? I doubt you still have mine, but I want you to have yours back. I

used it down in the basement this morning, shad-
owboxing. It was sad, knowing it was the last day
I'll ever train, but it was a comfort, like you were
with me.

When Cord looked up, Liana was sitting next to him.
She put her hand in his. Tears pooled in his eyes. They
sat for a while, glad to be next to one another for whatever time they had left.

CHAPTER 23

So Mark had hypnotized Mercy too, somehow planted the idea that he and Cord should fight in the cage. The intricacy of Mark's plot astounded him. How long had this been in the planning? Two years? Five? Since Mark showed up on his doorstep that very first day?

"What if we get in the car," Liana asked, "and just keep driving?"

"It wouldn't do any good. You understand he's not human, right? That he doesn't follow normal physical laws? He can appear whenever and wherever he wants."

She put a hand to the back of her neck, felt the tattoo. "It's crazy. But I believe you. What about Father Reginald?"

"I've already talked to him. Christianity is sleeping this one off."

"Then, like I said before, our only option is Mark."

"If we can break the hypnotic spell, maybe I can get to him. Right now, it works like some kind of proximity detector. Last time I tried to drive out to his place, I got really sick and had to turn around."

"We'll talk to Keoni tomorrow."

"Okay. But it has to be before the fight."

"What fight?"

"I have a cage-fight tomorrow."

She whirled. "Are you crazy? The last place you should be is inside a cage. You might as well just hand yourself over to the demon."

"I have to face him, anyway. At least this way, it's on my turf."

Cord didn't believe it himself, but he felt it was important she didn't give up hope. With the one glove, he might be able to take the demon with him to the grave. That is, if demons were even capable of dying. Cord hoped they were.

Otherwise, he was fucked.

"Dean Masland, that's the dumbest thing you've ever said. And believe me, I've heard you say some pretty dumb things over the years."

"I'm a fighter, Li."

"Now you sound like Vic. And he's dead. The two of you—I swear, you're the two most stubborn men I've ever met."

"I'll take that as a compliment."

"Take it however you want. And go to your stupid fight, but I'm coming with you."

"The hell you are," he said. "You're going to stay

with Lovie and Senator. Far away from that grizzly bastard."

"I'm coming with you."

He rolled his eyes. "Liana, you hate MMA. You never came to one of my fights."

"Yeah, well, that's about to change."

"Yo," Lovie interrupted from behind, "matching tattoos. Cool."

Cord's hand flew unconsciously to the back of his neck. He was surprised to see Liana's hand do the same. "Don't you have somewhere to be, Lovie?"

"One minute you're broken up, now you're getting inked-up together."

"Let's not get started on tattoos, Lovie. Unless you want to lift up your shirt and show us your Mindy Shepherd tribute?"

Lovie tucked in his upper lip, pivoted, and stormed off.

"He still carries that torch, huh?"

"Nine years now, the idiot. He's put his life on hold for some girl who probably doesn't even remember he exists."

"Isn't that a little harsh?"

"That guy," Cord said, jerking his thumb in the direction of the kitchen, "is going to wake up somewhere down the line and wonder why he wasted his twenties. He still thinks about her all the time, and when he's not, he's getting fucked up trying *not* to think about her. To him she's become a deity. If he ever actually saw her, he'd probably drop to his knees and pray."

"I'm right here," Lovie said from the kitchen. "I can hear you."

"Let's get out of here," Cord said. He grabbed his keys off the table.

"Where to?"

"Anywhere."

It was a warm evening. The sun had just slipped below the horizon, leaving lines of polished gold at the skyline. As he pulled out of the driveway, Cord shot a glance into the woods, now a black outline of skeletal branches. He thought he saw movement—a hulking form—but it might've been one of the oaks guarding the property.

He drove without direction, feeling his way along the winding roads. All the way, the Coroner tracked them. Cord saw him now and then, standing at the edge of the highway, or off in the embankment past the shoulder. Once, he saw him sitting atop the median guardrail, arms-crossed, lab coat flying out behind him. If Liana saw him, too, she didn't let on. She remained silent, staring out the window.

Cord pondered the riddles Senator had offered. Ring, moon, octopus. What was the connection? There were so many things he had yet to understand, and now it was nearly too late. One thing *was* certain: he would try to save Liana, no matter the cost. The thought gave him a strange chill—not of fear, but grim resignation. His fate appeared to have been sealed long ago, years before, as Senator had read in the Tarot cards.

But when would he have the chance to save her? And how? He slipped his hand into his pocket. Before they'd left, he'd grabbed the engagement ring he'd kept in his drawer. It had to be *this* ring the riddle prophesied. But what to do with it? He glanced out the window at the full moon cresting the horizon. And where, besides Sea-World, had he seen an octopus before?

In a flash, the answer came to him. He thought of Mercy's letter, and it all fell into place. He turned off the main road and after a few miles got onto the Taconic. He drove south with Liana asleep in the seat next to him.

CHAPTER 24

Sterling Lake. At dusk, they parked at the octopus playground near Cord's old house. The moon was dusty-red and full, hanging low on the horizon. The streetlights crackled and buzzed, throwing a yellow-orange glow over the pavement. He sat on the hood, scanning the area for the Coroner. The demon gave no sign he was around. Maybe they'd gotten lucky and hell had an influx of new corpses that needed dissecting, Cord thought. Life and death press on, two kindred spirits.

"My favorite cephalopod," Liana said, walking over to the slides. "When was the last time we were here?"

"Four years ago."

"Why are you smiling?"

"Do you remember the last time? In the middle of the night?"

"*That* time?"

One night they'd gotten bored and went for a walk at

two in the morning. They'd never slept much when they were together—six years of lost sleep, the best years of his life. Liana had suggested they climb down into the octopus's spongy foam core. He wasn't sure whose idea it'd been to take their clothes off, but one thing led to another, down there, under ten feet of apparatus.

He couldn't hold back a laugh. It was catchy, and soon Liana was clutching his shoulder, hauling in wheezy breaths. He wiped at his eyes. When the last of the giggles subsided, they were both sitting on the ground, backs to one of the purple slides. She squeezed his hand. He glanced down, surprised to see she wore the silver bracelet on her wrist. She said, "I can't believe we did that."

"I can," he said. "You always liked public places—bathrooms, movie theaters, golf courses—"

"Oh, like any of that was my idea."

"What about Woodside, on top of one of the mausoleums?"

She gave him her cynical smile. "Maybe that one time."

They walked toward the lake. Cord brought along the fighting glove, stuffed in his back pocket, just in case the Coroner appeared out of the shadows. Liana's lilac perfume filled his nostrils. He let her walk ahead a little to check out the way her low-cut jeans hugged her ass, her short T-shirt pulling up to expose the butterfly tattoo on her lower back.

The lake was a swath of rippling blackness. The hum of the cicadas grew steadily louder, increasing in urgency, a high-frequency sonic warble. They took the trail that led down to the water's edge, ending at the area near the weeping willows where he'd brought her the first time. Cord realized that, although they'd visited the lake many times after that first, they'd never returned to this particular spot.

The lake writhed in inky blackness, lapping at the craggy shoreline, pushing through the cattails and spikes of horsetail rush. The weeping willows stooped ten feet from the water's edge like hoary old men, tree trunks for canes, leafy beards drooping to the ground. The moon dragged a trail of white jewels across the lake's rippled surface.

Liana kicked off her sandals, dipped her toes in the water. "It's cold."

He felt content, watching her stand near the moonlit path. When he used to watch her perform Shakespeare, he knew the outcome. He used to think he knew their life-script as well. But they'd taken a wrong turn, had forgotten their lines. Looking at her now—a solitary figure swallowed by the immense backdrop of the lake—he realized that, although his destiny seemed to be set, he had no idea as to the outcome of this particular performance. Their lives were, for the first time, unscripted. He hadn't needed Senator's palm reading to know that, since they first met, their destinies had been intertwined. Screw the expiration dates, he thought. Their lives were what they would make of them.

She pulled off her T-shirt, shimmied out of her jeans, and took something out of her pocket. He was already walking toward her, hauling off his own clothes.

She looked great in her white lacy bra and bikini-cut panties, her lithe body and pale skin in soft contrast to the rolling blackness of the watery surface. He should've been cold, standing in his boxers, but he wasn't. So close, he felt her heat.

"Do you remember the promise?" she asked.

He nodded then closed his eyes. This time, the vision came to him immediately. He envisioned a path of liquid mercury with a solid sheen of metal beneath the water's surface.

"Can you picture it?" she whispered.

He squeezed her hand, once. His breath steamed out of his mouth, his pulse a thunderous drumbeat in his ears. "One. Two. Three…"

They both stepped forward.

He slipped the ring onto her finger. Then…

❧❧❧

He watches Liana crying in her apartment, looking at wallet-sized pictures of her half-sisters on the desk. She's trying to figure out how to kill Ralph Worth, how to get away with murder. Cord calls, but she doesn't answer, ignores his message. She can't stop thinking about Mark, the things he told her. Cord—her best friend in the world, the one she'd trusted above anyone—had betrayed her.

Then she's out the door, her car slipping through the oily-black streets—the hard rain from earlier settling into a slow drizzle. She needs to talk to someone. Anyone but Cord. She's so angry, she's afraid of what she might do, how she might act. All those expectations. Marriage. Kids. Moving away together. All a fantasy, she thinks. An infantile delusion.

She drives to Mercy's house. His car is there. She disliked him at first—his loud mouth, his wild attitude. Cord always acted reckless around Mercy—selfish, obsessed with living in the moment.

But over the years, Mercy had grown on her. He hadn't made Cord the way he was. Mercy would lie down in front of a bus for Cord if asked. He often invited them over for dinner, spent entire nights as waiter and chef, serving them without sitting down to eat himself.

Mercy answers the door. "Here's a surprise," he slurs.

He's drunk. An empty Smirnoff pint and drained beer cans litter the table. "Kelly came over earlier, and we got into it," he explains.

"Geez, did you break up?"

He stifles a belch with the back of his hand. "Looks that way."

"What happened?"

He shrugs. "She can't wait for me any longer."

Liana realizes she's absently playing with the silver bracelet on her wrist and forces herself to stop, thinking, *When did I put this thing on?* "How long have you guys been together?"

"On-and-off since high school. The thing is I'm a fighter. I've got a bunch of fights lined up, Cord, too. That's not really conducive to a relationship."

He barely gets the words out.

"Vic, you're a mess. You should go to bed."

He nods dumbly.

Upstairs, she helps him peel off his beer-soaked shirt, and by this point, he's already half-comatose. She gets him a glass of water, noticing an octopus magnet on the fridge, oversized beak protruding in a dumb grin. She returns with the water and a damp washcloth for his forehead, which is slicked with sweat.

She bends to put the washcloth on his forehead, and he grabs her wrist, pulls her down toward him. "I'm sorry, babe," he says. "C'mere." He pulls her in and kisses her. He tastes of stale beer and potato chips. She shoves him off.

"Vic." In a few seconds, he's snoring. She shuts off the lights and leaves...

☙❧❧

The ring slipped off Liana's finger, fell into the lake. Pain lanced through the tattoo on Cord's neck. The feel of needles stabbing his skin.

He remembered the promise he'd made her seven years before: *Promise me you'll take back this bracelet, if ever I offer it to you.*

It seemed a harmless assurance at the time. Why would he ever have to take it back? Now, though, he knew what she was doing, and she was almost done. The final symbol wasn't the ring, it was the bracelet she held in her hand. She slipped it over his wrist—

His eyes flew open, and he snatched the bracelet off his wrist, slipped it over her arm, held it there.

"No!" she screamed.

The moonlit path disappeared beneath him, and he plummeted. Liana grabbed for him, but it was no use. He plunged into the icy water. He saw her body from below, as through a thick pane of distorted glass. Her skin a cream-white halo against the obsidian sky. Her outstretched hands reaching toward him, the bracelet coiled around her arm. Then she vaulted off the path and onto dry ground as he exploded through the surface.

He groped his way up the bank and choked out a few watery coughs, feeling like he'd inhaled a gallon of icy lake water. When the coughing ceased, he lay on his back staring up at the stars, the bright pinpricks of light perforating the inky-black curtain of space.

"Are you okay?"

"Fine, babe."

"You broke your promise," she said. "How *could* you?"

"I couldn't let you do it. I couldn't take it back." He grabbed her hand, ran his fingers over the bracelet on her arm—silver beads catching the moon's rays, reflecting the ashy light. "C'mere," he said, his teeth chattering, "let me see." He touched the back of her neck—and found unblemished skin.

She ran her fingers along the back of her neck. "It's gone, isn't it?"

He nodded. "It was the bracelet. Somehow being on that path, wearing the bracelet—it removed the curse."

"What about yours?"

"Still there."

"We can try again," she said, getting up and heading toward the water.

"No," he said. "It won't work again." Senator had been right. Their destinies were intertwined. One of them would survive, not both.

She stared out over the lake. Then she nodded. "C'mon then." She led him to the largest willow. She pulled him on top of her, onto the fallen boughs that carpeted the space underneath. With her to guide him, he had no trouble finding his way in the dark.

CHAPTER 25

Afterward, they felt a breeze on their naked flesh, but mostly it was warm in the sheltered space beneath the tree. Any other time he'd be breaking out in a cold sweat in the tight enclosure, but now, beside Liana, he felt fine.

"All this time, you thought that…" Liana began.

"Vic told me."

"He told you? I'm surprised he even remembered kissing me."

"He remembered. That and a lot more."

"But that's all that happened. A drunken kiss, and he thought I was Kelly."

"I don't know, Li. I really thought you guys hooked up that night."

"How could you think he would? That *I* would?"

"Well, he said you did. Also, you basically went out of your way to avoid me after that. What was I supposed to think?"

"No. I was really hurt that you would've told everyone about my stepfather, but I avoided you because of the palm reading, the one Senator did right before everything got so crazy between us."

Cord shook his head. "I didn't take that seriously. I blew it off, didn't give it a serious thought. Until now."

"I did. A lot. That day on the lake when you first gave it to me? I had this really crazy vision that one day this bracelet—" She held it up, the beads glinting faintly in the dim moonlight filtering through the boughs. "—would protect us somehow. One of us, anyway. But I also saw that you would die trying to save me. But then I thought that if I did things just right, made you take it back at just the right time, you'd live, too. That's why I had you make that promise. But then I got scared and thought that if we separated completely—then whatever it was couldn't get us at all."

"So then you dumped me."

She nodded. "Essentially."

"Thanks."

"Well, geez, Cord. Could you have dealt with that knowledge and stayed together?"

"I don't know, Li."

"I wasn't going to risk us being together and making that vision come true."

"So you split. But then Vic died. And I came back into your life."

She nodded. "And then when I heard Senator with that riddle, I knew it had to be tonight. I knew I had to recreate whatever magic I had on that first day at the lake.

I knew what was after you. I saw him—*it*—myself. I had to try to save you with the bracelet. But you went ahead and fucked it all up." She kicked his leg. "Jerk."

"You heard the riddle?"

She nodded. "I listened in the hallway."

"I should've figured."

"What do we do now?"

"Now?" he asked. "We get dressed and find Keoni."

ↄﾟↄﾟↄﾟ

She was attending High Falls' Tenth Annual Samādhi Campout. She'd been in meditation for a good part of the night. She wasn't supposed to receive phone calls, she told Liana, but she agreed to meet them on top of Lookout Hill, a few miles down the Taconic.

Lookout Hill was one of the highest points in High Falls. Cord exited at Route 6 and drove a few miles before the GPS chimed, indicating a winding dirt road that led off into the woods and up a steep hill with trees pressed tight on either side.

"What have we got to lose?" Cord circled up the hill, winding around in a constant arc. Branches scraped at the sides of the car. He was glad for the dark. He didn't want to see the drop-off over the unguarded sides of the road, a near-vertical plunge in some places. What would happen if a car came the other way? *Hell if I'm going to back all the way down this monster.*

"Are you okay?" Liana asked.

"Yeah, why?"

"The way you're gripping the steering wheel. Look at your knuckles."

His knuckles were bone-white. He forced himself to relax, concentrating on the sweep of the headlights over the stony path, pretending they were on a flat expanse.

Near the top, the trees retreated to a clearing and a parking lot edged by a guardrail overlooking the greater part of the Hudson Valley. A few cars were parked along the rail. Cord maneuvered the Celica into a spot and got out, creeping over to the edge. Liana joined him, both of them taking in the view.

Gleaming light punctuated a sky of black velvet , and in the folds, hulking shapes crowded over the horizon: the Bearkill Mountains. The valley opened beneath them like a gouge carved out of the Earth, the trees in the foreground opening up and retreating down the steep incline until only the tops were visible.

The Hudson River snaked through the foliage in the distance, its rippled surface reflecting the moonlight high overhead, transforming it into a serpent made of liquid mercury. Lights dotted the countryside beyond, thousands of flickering candles in the dark, the glimmer of humanity.

"It's beautiful," Liana said.

It would've been breathtaking if Cord had had any breath to take. He'd been wheezing for most of the ascent.

He held up a finger and retreated away from the edge, regaining his breath. "It's amazing," he said. "But it's better from over here. Where is she?"

"They're camping in the woods. She said she'd be at the fire tower at ten."

He looked at his watch: nine-fifty. "Where's the fire tower?"

She pointed across the clearing to a broken-down structure above a bed of craggy limestone at the edge of a cliff. It might once have been a fire tower but was now a series of rusted metal supports and a set of skeletal stairs leading to nowhere.

"I'm not climbing that."

Liana laughed. "At the *base* of the tower."

They crossed the clearing. "You sure she's coming?" Cord asked, again checking the time.

"She said she'd be here. And she's a Buddhist. She keeps her promises."

Finally, they heard rustling at the edge of the clearing and saw a figure emerge through a path in the woods, holding a candle. Keoni had on the traditional triple-layered Tibetan robes, a solid maroon color that looked like claret in the candlelight. "I hope you have a good reason for pulling me away from my meditations on the *Ariya*. Not to mention I'm missing out on the *zhāicài* cookout, and I've been fasting all day."

"It's important."

"I suppose Nirvana only comes to those able to abolish selfishness and craving," Keoni said with a sigh. "Buddha once said, 'Liberated, the wise are indifferent to the senses and have no need to seek anything; passionless, they are beyond pleasure and displeasure.'"

"I'm glad you're on the fast track to Nirvana," Cord

said. "I'm on the express train to warmer southern climates."

"We need your help, Keoni. We're in trouble."

Keoni's eyes widened. "Oh, that reminds me. I performed your urinalysis."

"And?"

"After vigorous stirring, I noticed the persistence of white bubbles with a bottom deposit of soot. Also, the color exhibited a greenish hue and smelled strongly of—"

"What does his pee—"

"Let her finish," Cord said.

"I was able to confirm the shadow of a demonic presence in your body as well as a localized infection, most likely stemming from hypnotic aggression."

"That's amazing, Keoni," Liana said. "Can you remove the hypnotic trance?"

"I'm afraid I'm not skilled in the hypnotic arts. However, it may be unnecessary." Keoni pulled out a plastic bag filled with greenish-brown leaves, crushed buds, and stems.

"Are you sure now's a good time to spark up?" Cord asked.

"It's not marijuana. It's a mixture of *nardostachys jatamansi* and *terminalia chebula*. Sprinkle the mixture in a gallon of water. Steep and serve. Three glasses should do the trick."

"That'll cure the curse?"

"The curse, I'm afraid, is beyond my abilities. This should remove the adverse hypnotic effects for a brief period of time."

"How brief?"

Keoni shrugged. "An hour, two at the most. It's the best I can do."

Cord took the bag.

"Thanks, Ki," said Liana.

"I have to get back."

"Any chance there's a healer on the mountain who could help?"

"Possibly. Though most of the elders here have retreated to their huts, where they go to smoke the *calea zacatechichi* to induce a dreamlike state. They're likely naked. It's part of the symbolic act of shedding possessions."

Cord considered for a moment. "I've seen enough saggy old man parts to last me a while."

❦

On the way back, they stopped off at a convenience store for hot water and dispersed the herbal mixture into a Styrofoam cup. While they waited in the car for the tea to steep, Liana said, "You think this will work? Sometimes Keoni can be kind of flighty."

"I need to believe in something, Li. Or else I might as well give up now."

"How will we know if it works?"

"I'm going to drive straight to his house. Trust me, we'll know."

"Then what?" Liana asked. The headlights of a passing car reflected in her eyes. "Beat him up? Kill him? Spend the rest of your life in prison?"

"Isn't that a bit hypocritical? You were just saying earlier how you wanted to punch him in the face."

"That was earlier. Now, it just sounds ridiculous, the violence."

"You sound like your mother."

She stared out the passenger window.

"What do you want me to do?" he asked. "Either Mark will win—and the demon will kill me—or I'll get to him first. It's that simple. Maybe I won't kill him, but I can sure beat some fear into him."

"What if he can't undo whatever he did?"

"He'll have to."

"Let me save you," she said, holding up her wrist to show the bracelet. "With this."

He sensed, somehow, that the bracelet had acted as a kind of talisman that had protected Liana from the curse. He didn't know exactly how and didn't much care as long as she was safe. He remembered Senator's prophecy and knew he couldn't take the bracelet back. It would put her life in danger. He couldn't risk it, not even if she wanted him to. "I can't take it back."

"You made a promise."

"Screw the promise. Just don't take it off, okay? And try not to leave it in the garbage disposal this time."

They sat in silence for a few minutes, watching the late-night traffic sweep down the highway. Finally, he said, "Tea's ready. Cross your fingers."

೧৩৩

They drove toward Mark's development. Cord wanted her to drive, in case Keoni's remedy didn't work. If he became violently ill, like the day of the funeral, she could turn around and head the other way.

"This," he said, pointing at a Walgreens, "is as far as I got last time."

Liana edged off the gas and the car crept forward. Up ahead was a shopping plaza. His stomach muscles writhed in anticipation, and he held his breath, ready for the gut-wrenching nausea. They passed the Ames that'd been vacant since Cord was a child, and soon the plaza faded from view and there was the open road.

"Well?" she asked.

"I feel fine."

Liana gave him an uneasy smile. "I'm glad."

They drove on.

 espeis

They parked on the street in front of a modern Colonial with a driveway like a jet runway and a manicured front lawn as big as a football field. The Colonial was a hulking two-story edifice that seemed to tell the neighbors *what you can do, I can do bigger*.

Mark, with his wife and two kids, didn't need a mansion, but he wanted someplace to show off his Restoration Hardware furniture and New York City art.

"Stay here," Cord said.

"No way."

"Li, if things go wrong, I need you to have the car running."

"We're not robbing a bank, Cord. This isn't a getaway vehicle. If something goes wrong, I want to be with you."

"Li—"

"Last time I checked," she said, opening the door, "your brother was trying to kill me, too."

Cord checked his watch: *midnight*. Too late, he guessed, for Mark to be up looking out the window. They might make it to the front door without being spotted, but he had no idea what he'd do when he got there. He wasn't much for game plans.

In his fights, he'd always performed better when he relied on instinct.

He recalled the words of Bruce Lee: '*The consciousness of the self is the greatest hindrance to the proper execution of all physical action.*'

Forethought got in the way of intuition; planning undermined the spontaneity of reaction. *Besides,* he thought, *plans only work until you took the first shin to the skull. After that, it's all instinct, anyway.*

Liana grabbed his arm. "We can't just ring the doorbell."

"Actually, that's not a bad idea."

The sensor light over the garage flared to life, bathing the driveway and lawn with a glaring-white light. So much for the element of surprise, Cord thought. A sheet of paper was taped to the door.

> *My Dear Brother,*
> *Better luck next time.*
> *~ Mark*

Cord handed the note to Liana. He went around to the garage and peered inside. It was empty.

"We could break in," Liana suggested.

"No use. He's gone." Cord clutched his stomach. It suddenly felt like an army of worker ants was chewing at his gut. "And the nausea's back."

As they drove away, Cord worked over his options. By the time they reached the Taconic, he realized he didn't have any.

He looked at his watch: *after midnight.*

His expiration date had arrived.

EXPIRATION DATE...

CHAPTER 26

Cord woke at home with Liana in bed beside him. He slid his arms around her and pulled her close, kissing the bare skin on her neck where the tattoo had been the night before. At first he thought it was a dream, her warm body, her wonderful scent. Over the last two years, such dreams had come with increasing frequency. Instead of waking to her warmth pressed against his skin, he would reach out only to find an empty bed. It was ironic. Now it was finally real, and all he could think was how soon it would be over.

He slid out of bed, a feeling of electric anticipation running through him. The time for questioning, for blundering around playing detective, was over. He'd never make a good sleuth anyway. It was time to fight. Ever since he'd opened that e-mail, he'd known he would attend the *Fight Like Hell* tournament. He wasn't stupid. This was where he would fight for his life. He and Mercy had this in common—if they could choose how they would go out, it would be inside an octagon cage.

Liana stretched, yawned, and regarded him with a drowsy smile. It was like watching his last sunrise, the most beautiful thing he could imagine. "What time is it?"

"Eight."

"What time is the event?"

"Two o'clock." He would probably be among the first to fight, which was good—get it out of the way early, before the jitters got bad. He had to win three fights to get to the final. It was nothing new. He'd competed in these tournaments before. He felt confident he would win his matches, no matter his opponent. But at some point in the day, he would be fighting for more than a pro card.

Liana knelt at the edge of the bed. "You don't seem very concerned."

"There's nothing left to do. Mark is gone. I have to fight."

"This is not a normal fight, and you know it. Listen, it's not too late to call it off. All we have to do is wait until midnight. We could find somewhere to hide—"

"I'm not hiding, and I'm not running. It wouldn't help, anyway."

"So you'll get yourself killed in that cage. To prove what?"

"I'm not trying to prove anything. I stand a better chance in the cage than anyplace else."

"You talk like you're already dead," she argued. Cord saw the anger drain from her face, leaving only resignation. "We don't have much time," she concluded.

He nodded, content to linger in her presence, to take in the soft arch of her hips, the fullness of her breasts.

"Come here," she said.

He slid into bed, his hands finding her body.

✂✄✂

He zipped up his bag, stood, and peered at the fish tank, the azure-blue water choked with fake ferns and water lilies. Lulu meandered around the perimeter of the tank, the sole survivor. All his other fish—blood fin tetras, rummy noses, silver hatchet fish—were dead. Some lay in pieces at the bottom among the multi-colored aquarium gravel; some floated at the top like chum, something you'd throw in the water to attract a bigger fish. He frowned, moved toward the glass. Lulu peeked out at him from behind a chunk of rock coral, her dark eyes accusing him of abandonment.

"Do me a favor, Li," he said. "If something happens, take care of Lulu—"

"I'm not listening to this," she said, shoving off the bed and heading toward the door.

Downstairs, Lovie collared him in the hall. "C'mere, buddy," he said, motioning him through the kitchen to the screened-in back porch. "I want to show you something."

Rain drummed the siding, pelting the lawn like a herd of horses. A torrent spilled off the wooden overhang. Seeing out was like trying to peer through a waterfall. Lovie kicked out a chair for Cord to sit, slumped into the one opposite.

"Make this quick, Lovie," Cord said. "I've got a fight in Edison."

"I know. It's what I want to talk to you about." An open bag of M&Ms rested on the table, and Lovie dug in, grabbing a heaping fistful. He opened his mouth and fired one off his upper lip. "I'm not sure you should go. With everything that's going on—that creep hanging around, and with what happened with Mercy—I got a bad feeling."

"Lovie, where's this coming from?"

"I guess after this scare with my eye—it looks better, huh?" Lovie pulled down his lower eyelid, and Cord thought his eye did indeed look better. The milky-white discoloration was draining away, leaving more of the natural blue. "I got to thinking that life is kinda short, you know? I'm almost thirty. I'm unemployed."

"And you're realizing this now?"

"A couple of the things you've said lately really hit home," Lovie said, shoving a few more M&Ms into his maw. "I got to get past Mindy Shepherd, somehow. Maybe hypnotherapy—"

"How about a job?"

"Check this out." Lovie pulled up his shirt. The tattoo of Mindy Shepherd's face had been replaced by Jar Jar Binks, elephant ears, alien eyes on stalks. "I hate *Star Wars*," he said. "But it was the only thing they had big enough to cover over her face."

"That's a step in the right direction."

"Cord, that bearded dude ain't anybody's pal. If you're in money trouble, I can help you scrape together whatever you need. In the meantime, I ain't no fighter like you, but I can hold my own. Better the fight be here with your friends around than in some cage, don't you think?"

For a moment, Cord was speechless. Lovie hadn't spoken like that since college, back when he still had his drinking and drugging under control. Back then, Lovie had wanted to be a member of the Peace Corps, live in small villages among natives in foreign lands. None of that had panned out, of course. Such things often don't. But there was still time. If not for Cord, then for his friends.

Cord rose and put a hand on Lovie's shoulder. "What you just said—it meant a lot. It was like listening to my old bud again. Remember how we used to chill out on Sunday afternoons?"

"I wanted to help build schools for kids."

"You're still that person, brother," Cord said. "The one with those crazy-good ideas. Nothing's changed, just maybe you lost sight of those things for a while."

Lovie nodded. "But you're still going to go, huh? Then I'm coming with."

"No. Liana will be with me," Cord said. "And with all my gear, there's no room in the car. I'll see you when I get back."

He left Lovie sitting on the porch, framed by the backdrop of the rain pouring down in a cascade from the roof. Cord closed his eyes so he could remember the image.

CHAPTER 27

The New Jersey Civic Center looked like it was decorated for a porno convention, not an MMA event, with pink carpeting, fake-crystal chandeliers, a banquet hall with burgundy curtains that ran the length of the walls. Cord and Liana advanced to the entrance, shoving through a cloud of smoke from the lit cigarette of a white-haired codger leaning against the building's façade. They were greeted by a balding middle-aged man wearing a silver bowtie and a tight-fitting suit whose sleeves barely reached mid-forearm.

"Are you here for the Sally Mae Functional Literacy Program?" he asked.

"Yeah, I'm packing all this gear for the Women's Rotary," Cord said. "The amateur tournament."

The man's smile sagged. "Down the hall, three rights and then a left."

On the way, they passed a group of teenage girls

wearing identical Conor McGregor T-shirts and bright pink Clubwear mini-skirts. Next they strode by a man whose face was comically bandaged—all he had were two eyeholes cut out of the gauze to see through. He was shirtless and shoeless, wore MMA gloves and Tapout shorts, was pounding his fists together, grunting, and pacing up and down the hall. *If the doctors cleared* that *guy,* Cord thought, *I should have no problem.*

"What have you gotten me into?" Liana whispered.

They pushed into the reception area—a group of people milling about a room barely larger than a confessional—and spoke to a woman who directed them toward an anteroom where they would await the doctor for medical clearance. Cord wasn't surprised to see the same old codger they'd passed outside on their way in, still smoking a cigarette. His glasses sat crooked on the bridge of his nose. He'd only bothered to tuck one side of his shirt into his pants. He wore the cardinal sin: white sneakers and socks with dress pants.

Cord felt the rough pads of the doctor's fingertips, singed from his battle with nicotine addiction, prodding his face—the broken nose, the bandaged facial cuts, the bruised jaw.

His breath smelled rank. He breathed with a hitch and wheeze that reminded Cord of an overworked motor about to crap out.

"Open your mouth," the doctor said. Cord did and felt a brittle snap inside his head, a shooting pain in his jaw. "Does it hurt when I press here?" The doctor pressed into the tender spot at the edge of his jaw line.

Cord stifled a cry. It felt like someone was drilling into his skull. "No," he said. "Not at all."

"How about the nose?" the doctor said, tapping the bridge lightly with a small rubber hammer, normally used to test for reflexes.

Cord wiped away the tears streaming down the sides of his face. "Never better."

"These cuts don't look too good, but I don't think they will impede your vision. How do you feel?"

"Awesome, doc. Ready to rumble."

The doctor scribbled something down on a medical clearance form. "I'll tell you the same thing I told all of the other nuts who came in here today," he said, his face a sagging mass of wrinkles. "Knock 'em dead."

"That's exactly what I was planning to do," Cord said.

First up at two p.m.: Dean "Corduroy" Masland vs. Tobias "Lockjaw" Holmes. *Lockjaw*, Cord thought. Someone pointed him in the direction of the trainer's room. He hoped his trainer, Gears, was there. If not, Liana would have to wrap his hands.

He looked at his watch: *twelve-thirty*. He had an hour-and-a-half to suit up. Liana went to find something to eat, so he made his way to the trainer's room alone. On the way, Cord got his first look at the event room. Above the cage, a yellow banner hung from the ceiling: *The Edison Civic Center welcomes you to the First Annual FIGHT LIKE HELL Amateur MMA Tournament!!! Please present your tickets at the door.* Chandeliers glittered overhead, pastoral artwork hung from the walls, partially obscured by velvety curtains draped from the ceiling. Folding chairs had been lined up in butterfly rows on each side of the octagon. The floor was on a slight incline, which gave the marginal appearance of "stands."

He found the trainer's room and slipped inside, relieved to see Gears. "What took you so long, Jimmy?" Gears shouted, his voice deafening in the close confines of the bandbox room. "I was beginning to think you weren't going to show."

"Relax, tough guy."

"Sixteen fighters. That means you need four wins," Gears yelled.

"Obviously."

"You're gonna be the guy who walks out with that belt."

"There's no belt, Gears."

"You know what I mean. Now sit down." Gears weaved the gauze around his wrist then over the thumb, palm, through the knuckles. "I don't know much about your opponent, this *Lockjaw*, but the word is he's got a *glass* jaw. I want you to feint with the jab, throw a few leg kicks to set him up." Gears yelled loud enough for his opponent to hear them in the adjoining room. "Then when you're good and ready, fake low and go high." Gears was shaking, the cords in his neck standing out, sweat beads springing out on his forehead. You'd think *he* was the one getting ready to get into the cage. Cord tuned him out. Gears was marginally helpful under normal circumstances. Useless today. Cord knew what he was up against.

After wrapping both hands, Gears left to find a water bucket. Cord put on his corduroy shorts with his name in bold white lettering along the sides. Most MMA fighters had shorts made of a polyester/cotton blend—lightweight and great for absorbing moisture. Cord's were cumbersome and *not* particularly absorbent. But they were his good luck charm. If he could run into a burning building wearing corduroys and come out unharmed, he could survive fifteen minutes in a cage with them.

He pulled Mercy's glove onto his right hand, slipped another glove over his left, and flexed his fists, molding the leather to his hands. He didn't match. So what.

Liana appeared in the doorway. "I had to run across the street for food, and on the way back I barged into a function down the hall, a bake-off for Cystic Fibrosis. I felt guilty and bought a pie. Now I feel sick."

"Jesus, Li," he said. "Take a breath."

"I don't know how you stand this. Why are you so calm?"

"It's called focus."

"This is not a normal fight, and I wish you'd stop pretending it was."

"What do you want me to do? Run around screaming?"

"Yes. Run right out of the building and then maybe we can figure out what to do next."

"Pop used to have this saying: 'Run from things long enough and running will feel like staying still.'"

"Your father, the sage. The same guy who slept with a drill saw under his pillow."

"The point is, time passes and then you wake up one day and realize you were so busy running you forgot to live. Then someone like me digs your grave. What's waiting for me in that cage has been after me my whole life."

Liana was silent for a moment. Then she pulled him close, whispered in his ear: "'For he today that sheds his blood with me, shall be my brother; be he ne'er so vile.'" Then she kissed his forehead. "Go get 'em, tiger."

CHAPTER 28

The hall was nearly empty—only the hardcores showed up for the prelims. A couple of fighters—amateurs—sat in the front row, anxious to check out the competition. One guy stood out because of his height and the scraggly beard: the Norseman that'd broken Cord's arm in that Atlantic City bar. He towered over the others, yellow beard dangling, scissored out in a forked design over the middle of his chest.

Jesus, Cord thought. That can't be Lockjaw, not unless he changed his name. He'd gone by The Mangler back then.

Gears yelled in his ear: "Let loose your inner warrior, you savage fucker."

As Cord passed the fighters in the front row, the Norseman made a motion like he was snapping a piece of dry kindling over his knee. But he made no move to take off his shirt or to get inside the cage. He was not Tobias

"Lockjaw" Holmes, a fact that did not sadden Cord in the least.

The ref—a kid who looked young enough to need a fake ID—checked him over, making sure he had a mouthpiece and a cup and that he hadn't doctored his gloves. Two years prior, an MMA fighter had taken all the padding out of the gloves before his fight. When he was done, his opponent looked like something you'd see in the supermarket meat case. He got caught—a permanent ban from the amateur and pro circuits—but lots of guys got away with such tricks. Anything for an advantage.

Cord entered the cage and went over to his "corner," although in an octagon, the term "side" would be a more accurate representation. When "Lockjaw" stepped in, Cord was surprised to see the same fighter they'd passed earlier in the hallway, the one who had his entire head bandaged. Now Cord saw why. His face was a swollen mess—stitches running up and down his cheeks, his nose bent at a thirty-degree angle. One look at him and Cord thought *Frankenstein*. Despite his facial injuries, Lockjaw snarled and jumped up and down, pointing at Cord and smacking himself in the face, meaty thwacks that resounded across the cage and echoed through the near-empty banquet hall. Nut-case, Cord thought.

When the ref brought them together and asked if they were ready to fight, a woman's voice shrieked from behind, shattering the silence: "Kill him, Corduroy!"

Cord peered around, finding Liana standing cageside, covering her mouth—*Oops, was that loud?*

The ref clapped once. "*Bring it on!*" he exclaimed, like Big John McCarthy.

The bell rang. They met in the center, tapped gloves, backed off. Cord heard a voice in the back of his mind, and it wasn't Gears, but Lao, who told him, '*The first one to the dance always gets a date. Be first.*' Cord came forward and threw a left cross that hammered into Lockjaw's face, ripping open the stitching and releasing runners of blood down his cheeks. Lockjaw fired back with a mid-counter that caught Cord in the ribs, forcing a whoosh of air from his lungs. Cord grinned—nothing like a punch to the gut to wake you up. They circled for a bit, trading leg kicks, until Lockjaw shot for a takedown that Cord stifled with a double-underhook grapple and spin-off from the cage.

More voices. Sifu Lao, Ted Wong, Yip Man. They told him to let go of his ego. Cast aside all thought. Then the words of Bruce Lee carried loud above all others, and Cord listened.

'*Forget about winning and losing; forget about pride and pain. Let your opponent graze your skin and you smash into his flesh; let him smash into your flesh and you fracture his bones; let him fracture your bones and you take his life.*'

Cord felt himself synched with his opponent, anticipating his movements. When Lockjaw threw a jab, Cord slipped and countered to the jaw. When Lockjaw kicked, Cord checked and fired back a flurry: jab, jab, cross, uppercut. Lockjaw fell back against the cage, blood pouring out of half a dozen cuts. Cord let him rebound off the cage and shot off a high hook kick that seemed to hang suspended for an instant before crashing into Lockjaw's temple. His eyes rolled into his head and he swayed drunkenly, but he remained on his feet for another moment—his body hadn't registered that his mind had powered down and was initiating a reboot. Then his legs kicked out from under him and the back of his head smacked the canvas, body twisted in an awkward jumble of arms and legs. The ref immediately waved his arms, stating the obvious.

"Fight's over."

CHAPTER 29

Cord watched the rest of the first rounders from the front row, sitting between Liana and Gears. Gears kept up a clichéd monologue, "That guy might as well paint an X on his chin," which Cord tried to ignore.

The Norseman fought in the final first-round fight. He came into the cage in full Viking attire: steel breastplate and shoulder armor, iron leggings, Valkyrie helmet with brown eagle wings jutting from the sides. His beard reached nearly to the Viking crest—a warrior thrusting a sword into a sea serpent's belly. In one hand, he carried a gleaming double-headed axe, the handle embroidered with Norse symbols that Cord couldn't identify; in the other hand, a round wooden shield, two feet across. He charged around the cage, howling and clapping the axe against the shield, making a dull *thunk* sound. Cord had seen this act in the nightclub, though not on so grand a scale. He hoped the Norseman hadn't been working as hard on his training as he apparently had been on his stage presence. Liana shrank back and felt for Cord's hand. "That man is awful," she whispered.

"He's all show," Gears said.

Cord didn't contradict him. Then again, Gears hadn't been there that night in Atlantic City. Cord recalled the brittle snap of his arm as it gave way. He fought back the first real case of nerves he'd had all day. "'Forget about winning and losing,'" he intoned. "'Forget about pride and pain.'"

The Norseman faced a stocky Irishman, six foot, soft around the middle, thick legs, a Celtic cross tattooed on his back. The Irishman called himself Corey "Jelly" O'Callaghan. The Norseman was announced only as The Mangler. The ref brought the fighters to the center of the ring. "Gentlemen, you've already been given instructions in the dressing room. If you have any questions, ask them now, if not, touch gloves and come out fighting." When Jelly reached to touch gloves, the Norseman shoved the Irishman back onto his ass. The referee stepped between them. "Cut that out," he said, like a harried gym teacher.

"Cheap shot," said Gears.

At the bell, the Norseman came out bellowing in Norsk and, while it was impossible to understand what he was saying, his intentions were clear: "Make peace with your God because it is a fine day to die." Jelly didn't land a single blow. The Norseman hit Jelly with a series of overhand rights then a left uppercut to the gut. Finally, mercifully, Jelly fell onto his back and the Norseman jumped on top of him, securing his patented arm-bar by throwing his legs across Jelly's face and hyper-extending the arm across his hip bone. Jelly tapped, but the Norseman kept cranking. As the ref tried to pull him off, the Norseman screamed and tugged harder. The arm bent back, flaring at the elbow joint, and finally snapped, a sound that seemed to reverberate through the mostly-empty hall. People winced and turned away. The Norseman jumped to his feet, arms raised. Jelly, a bloody mess on the canvas, clutched his arm, curled into the fetal position.

Liana covered her face with her hands.

"Keeps his left a little low," Gears said.

❧❧❧

Cord's second fight was against a Muay Thai kickboxer who was all stand-up and no ground game. After taking a few knees to the gut from the clinch, Cord grabbed a leg and hauled the kickboxer to the ground. He struck a few elbows and knees to the ribs then latched onto the guy's arm in a kimura. The kickboxer tapped.

In the third match, Cord fought an aging Brazilian Jiu-jitsu ground specialist. The guy had no standup skills. His lurching movements reminded Cord of one of George Romero's zombies. Cord danced around the cage, staying clear of his opponent's range, peppering the grappler with jabs and leg kicks, setting up the cross. Several times the grappler shot in for a takedown, but each time Cord stuffed the attempt and spun away, landing blow after blow to the grappler's face. Soon the guy had one eye swollen and a hematoma bulging like a cancerous growth from his forehead, and Cord nailed him with a knee to the jaw that sent the grappler sprawling to the canvas. Second round KO.

Now, Cord sat by himself on the bench in the trainer's room. He checked his watch: *eleven p.m.* An hour left and still no sign of the Coroner. If he could make it to midnight—but no, he told himself. Don't look that far ahead. Focus on what's in front of you: a title match with the Norseman, a maniacal opponent, who'd already broken his arm once—and it wasn't even his chief concern at the moment.

Cord had a small cut on his forehead. Gears had gone to hunt down Avitene, petroleum jelly, and more ice, and Liana had gone with him.

Where was the Coroner? What was he waiting for? Cord sensed the demon was toying with him. *Bring it on,* Cord thought.

The door opened behind him and he turned, expecting Gears.

It was Mark.

CHAPTER 30

Mark held out the photo of Cord being carried off after swatting his Little League homerun, and the nausea hit his gut. His knees buckled, muscles convulsing. *Not again,* he thought.

"You didn't think I'd miss the fight, did you? I've got a rooting interest in your competitor."

"The Norseman?" Cord managed.

"Not him," Mark said, a smile creasing his lips. "The other one."

A low moan escaped Cord, the only sound he could manage.

"What? I didn't catch that." Mark knelt down and tapped Cord in the forehead with the photo. "There are a few things I'd like to share with you before your next bout. Get up."

The nausea lessened, allowing him to think. Mark had told him to do something. Get up, he'd said. Cord opened his mouth to tell him off—but a strange thing happened. He rose and followed Mark to the door, down the hall, into a classroom-sized meeting room. Jade was seated at a small table, her bulk spilling over the edges of the chair. Her hair was purple all the way down to her scalp. She wiggled her fingers at him in a wave. "You don't look so well, dear."

"Sit," Mark said.

Cord sat. He knew he was hypnotized. How had he broken the trance before? Maybe he could summon the will to scream. He readied himself—

"Give me the glove on your right hand," Mark said.

Cord saw himself stripping off the glove and handing it to his brother, who put it on the table in front of Jade. She took off the pentacle she wore around her neck and placed it on the leather, mumbling an invocation in words that sounded like the Old English of *Beowulf.*

The glove trembled on the table, alive with a blue-white light that poured out from underneath. Then with a popping sound, it shorted out like an old bulb. A thin line of smoke curled into the air above the glove.

"There you go," Mark said. "Good as new." He held out the glove for Cord. A hole was burned through the leather.

Cord grimaced. Whatever magic the glove had held was gone.

"Do you remember how we used to talk about our lives being guided by a higher purpose? You never wanted to believe that there is a divine plan. I've had a lot of time to think about what you said, and I don't think I ever articulated myself properly. Do you remember that night out at Cayuga Lake?"

Jade shifted, the chair creaking beneath her. "Do we really need to rehash that right now?"

Mark threw her a nervous glance and continued, "Since that night, I've come to an important conclusion: God *does* have a plan. Some of us—you, for instance—are too ignorant to decipher the blueprint, and so you wade through life without a tether. You need guidance, Dean. That's the divine plan of some: to lead the less fortunate. You see, Dean, I spent my whole boyhood wondering why I suffered, why my own father rejected me, why my parents were taken from me so suddenly. I wondered what kind of god would allow such suffering. I cursed God in my anger, but He showed me a vision. He told me I had to suffer to find the truth. I saw my entire life flash in front of my eyes—I saw Jade, I saw our father, I saw you and Liana. I saw your friend Victor. God told me that they would be punished, but you—you, dear brother, might yet be saved. So I found a way to rescue your soul."

"The demon."

"I can't take complete credit for that." Mark gave Jade a sideways glance and patted her leg. "That was my wife's doing."

"I didn't even know I had it in me." Jade tittered, spots of red rising on her cheekbones.

"Jade was able to summon a representative from the other side. All we needed for completion of the, how shall I put it—"

"Charm spell," said Jade.

"Charm spell," Mark continued, "was a sacrifice."

"Mercy's death," Cord said. "And the photo of the fight. You were there that night."

"I took the picture. I saw the whole sordid affair."

"There was an invocation written on the back."

"One which you couldn't resist vocalizing," Mark said, checking his watch. "'With this, I will call forth the abyss to destroy my soul.'"

Cord could only nod. It felt like he was staring down at his own body, tethered by a thin rope, watching the action from a distance.

"Years ago, I made the decision to help you, since it became quite clear to me that you were not going to help yourself. Sin is an illness, Dean. Your relationship with Liana was nothing more than a disease."

"That bitch," Jade hissed.

Cord's mouth worked to find words, but no sound came out.

Mark made a waving motion with his hand: "Speak."

"How did you do it?"

"Simple. The old-fashioned way. I hired a private investigator. He discovered Ralph Worth's indiscretions with those girls."

Indiscretions, Cord thought.

"That was an interesting development. All part of a divine plan, I later realized. His death was a pleasant bonus, especially considering his means of execution, so to speak."

"Guess you had a change of heart about suicide."

"Au contraire, dear brother. For cretins like Ralph Worth, suicide is really the only option. Damned if you do, damned if you don't, I suppose."

"And you cursed Liana too?"

"We figured she must have been at least partially involved in Worth's death. He was her sacrifice, just like Victor was yours. It wasn't hard to get her to read the incantation—"

"We just left it in her mailbox!" Jade clapped her hand over her mouth to quell her outburst, her eyes darting manically between Cord and Mark.

"A little gift from us," Mark said, smirking. "Your girlfriend got in on the fun with you."

"You. Bastard."

"Trust me, Dean. She must have deserved it. It worked, didn't it?"

Jade wrinkled her nose. "That bitch probably spread her legs for half the men in this county!"

"Maybe so," Mark agreed.

Cord felt anger slicing like a hot knife through his gut. He focused all his energy and concentration on lunging across the table, wrapping his hands around his brother's throat.

The only thing he was able to move: his pinky. Barely.

Mark smiled. "Of course, the private investigator remained on the case—"

"Cost us a fortune, by the way," added Jade.

"He discovered Victor's brain condition. He was already damned anyway. I knew about his attempt to take his own life—the ultimate sin. 'If anyone destroys God's temple, God will destroy him; for God's temple is sacred, and you are that temple.' That's *Corinthians*, brother.

"I hoped that if you saw the effects of your actions firsthand—causing the death of your closest friend—you would stop the violence—"

"I'll kill you," Cord managed.

"In your condition? I highly doubt that," Mark said. "This fighting is why you never made anything of yourself. The reason why you're nearly thirty years old and still a gravedigger. Pop was also part of the divine plan, did you know? Before he died, he begged me to make you see the error of your ways."

"You're lying."

"It was his dying wish."

"Pop never asked me to quit fighting."

"He did, Dean, many times. You just didn't hear him." Mark pulled his chair closer, leaning in. "Listen, Pop only wanted the best for us. He was tough on us because he saw better things for our futures."

"He was a selfish asshole," Cord said.

"He did the best he could. God reunited me with Pop for a reason—to make me into the person I've become." A smile crept across Mark's face and lingered. It was a creepy thing to see, as unnatural as a pink bonnet on an MMA fighter. "I suppose it's time I let you in on a secret," he said, the smile seeming to harden on his face like cement.

Cord was silent. He didn't want to give his brother the satisfaction of seeing his curiosity.

"Remember that story I told you about my parents? The drunk driver jumping the rail? The head-on collision? Well, it didn't quite happen like that. Not *exactly*, anyway."

"What did you do?" Cord said.

"God wanted me to reunite with Stanley, and with you, brother. He came to me in a vision, showed me what needed to be done. My mother, you see, had always been weak. It was no wonder Pop didn't want anything to do with her. She should have fought to keep us together as a family, but she didn't even try. She gave up on him, let him walk away from us, from *me*, so effortlessly. I hated her for that. And when she met my *step*father—well, let's just say, I knew he would never substitute for the real thing. He and I never got along. He was married first to his job, second to his idiotic 'weekend warrior' outings, and third to my mother. Me, well, I didn't even rate.

"As a teenager, I began to loathe those two. Their weekend camping trips and their craft fairs, their flea markets. Their white picket fence. Their wholesomeness bored me to tears. And it was all a front. A white veneer that obscured the corruption beneath. I could tell they didn't love one another. Nor did they love me."

"What are you saying?"

"*Hypnosis*. That was the key to reuniting me with my true family, my true father, and you, my brother. I had been practicing for months, so I knew what to do. My stepfather gave me a pocket watch for my birthday. Fitting that I used it against him. One night, late after my mother had gone to bed, I tried it out. You know the turn on the Taconic past Cornwall? It seems to wind around forever—very narrow, very dangerous if you're not paying attention. I knew they were going out the next night and that they would take that route. Well, I *suggested* to him that, coming home, he would suddenly become quite tired—so tired, in fact, that he would fall asleep at the wheel around that very turn." Mark laughed, a sound that resembled a child being choked to death. "When the policeman showed up at the door—well, let's just say, I knew then the true power of persuasion."

"It was a drunk—" Cord said.

"The paper mentioned a drunk driver. It was little more than a blurb in the Sunday news. It hardly even rated as a story. Who cared? These things happened all the time. It's a dangerous road, an awful turn. Stanley certainly never questioned what happened. You remember only what I told you. No one but me knew what really happened that night. And I never told a soul, except for my wife—"

Cord's eyes flicked toward Jade, who sat motionless in her chair. "You knew about this?"

Jade flinched and looked away. She wrinkled her nose as if she just took a whiff of some unpleasant scent.

Perhaps it was her own evil stink, Cord thought. Hers and Mark's. For they were one and the same.

"I thought it important you should know," Mark continued. "So we don't have any secrets between us going forward."

"There is no *forward*, Mark. Don't you get that? I'm going to die in that fucking cage."

"The curse is meant to teach you a lesson—"

"He's not trying to scare me, Mark," Cord yelled. "He's trying to *kill* me. Don't you see what's written on the back of my neck?"

"Nonsense." Mark's gaze slid toward Jade. "That's ridiculous. Right, honey?"

Jade tried on a smile that—like her wardrobe—was one size too small. "These 'beings' are typically harmless. Ghosts can rarely take shape in this corporeal world—"

"*Ghosts?*" Cord sputtered. "You're telling me you don't know what you summoned?"

"What do you mean, brother?"

"You've sent the Coroner of *hell* after me." Cord saw only curiosity on Mark's face, but Jade recoiled in horror, her eyes widening.

"What's he talking about, dear?"

Jade tried to collect herself, but she couldn't stop her voice from shaking. "I sensed something different this time."

This time, Cord thought. How many times before had she interfered with others' lives? "You think this is some kind of game?"

"Silence," Mark said.

He threw Jade a questioning glance. She shook her head, almost imperceptibly, and Cord felt an almost-physical sensation of his own fate bearing down on him, ready to grind him to dust. "'From dust he had been de-livered; to dust he would return.'"

For once, he didn't need to defer to Mark about

scripture. He was an expert in that verse, having heard it spoken countless times over an open grave at Woodside Cemetery.

CHAPTER 31

Cord's eyes were open, but it felt as if he'd just woken from a nap. Gears stared down at him. "What the hell did you do to your glove?"

Cord looked down. He held Mercy's ripped glove in his hand. Through it he could see the far wall, the blowup of BJ Penn choking out some poor slob. "Hmm, I don't know." He felt like he had forgotten something vital. "Where's Liana?"

"Outside," Gears said, grabbing another glove.

"No, it has to be this one."

"Whatever you say." Gears pulled Mercy's glove over the tape on Cord's right hand. "So, are you ready? You're on in five." Without warning, Gears reared back and slapped Cord in the face.

Pain exploded through his injured nose. "The hell?"

"You need to wake the fuck up. You're staring at the biggest fight of your career, and you look like you just dragged yourself out of bed."

Cord rubbed his jaw. He had to admit he did feel more alert.

"The difference between a fighter and a champion," Gears said, inches from Cord's face, "is the champion knows how to push through the pain. This late, it's not physical anymore. It's all up here." Gears tapped Cord's forehead. "Either you find you got what it takes to be a champion, or you quit. And I don't train quitters—"

Cord tuned him out. He'd heard this pre-fight rant before—Gears delivered it word-for-word before almost every fight.

Liana appeared in the doorway, her face wan, dark hair clinging to her forehead. "I just got sick in the bathroom," she said. "I'm not cut out for this."

The event manager peered from the doorway. "Showtime, Masland."

Eleven-thirty. The title match set for five five-minute rounds. What Cord thought would be a sparse crowd had grown considerably since the opening bouts. Every seat was taken. There was standing room only—and stand they did, filling the aisles, the back rows, even the doorways. The crowd noise was louder than seemed possible for a small venue. It rattled through the floor and ran up through the metal stanchions and vibrated the cage.

Across the cage the Norseman glared at him. Cord's heart volleyed in his chest, seemingly intent on breaking through the walls of his ribcage. He focused on Bruce Lee's words: '*Empty your mind; be formless—shapeless, like water.*'

The ref called them over for the obligatory stare-down. *Here we go.* They met in the center of the octagon, the Norseman shoving his grizzly mug into Cord's face, baring a set of sharp yellow teeth and growling like a junkyard animal. His breath was terrible. When the Norseman jammed a forearm into his chest, Cord was ready. He grabbed the Norseman's arm and judo-threw *him* down on his ass. "Not this time, friend," he said.

The Norseman sprang back up, spitting, but the ref separated them. "Get back to your corners. And come out fighting when I say."

A few moments later, the ref held his hand up then dropped it like the flag at Daytona. *"Let's get it on!"*

The Norseman came out, throwing wild shots that Cord easily parried. He danced out of the way, feeling loose and relaxed. He was normally more of a stand-and-bang fighter, but because the Norseman outweighed him by fifty pounds, he concentrated on timing him, counter-punching. Let the Norseman tire himself out, he figured. As the Norseman lurched at him, Cord jabbed and got out of the way. He found his rhythm. Jab and dance. Soon, blood was dripping from the Norseman's nose.

The first round ended before Cord knew it, and the next round went much the same. The Norseman hadn't laid a finger on Cord yet, and Cord felt just as fresh after the second.

"You're picking him apart," said Gears. "Keep it up. His face looks like chopped meat. Keep sticking that jab! Stick it into his grill!"

Soon after the bell rang for the third round, the Norseman shot for a double-leg takedown, powered Cord to the ground, and fell on top of him, into side-control. The elbows rained down—splitting open his nose, again—and Cord felt the splash of warm blood on his cheeks. But he didn't panic. He'd been here before. He waited until the Norseman paused and then slipped into butterfly guard—his knees on the Norseman's hips, lower legs inside his thighs—and pushed off with his feet. But, as he sprang to his feet, the Norseman caught him with an elbow to his jaw. His vision quivered with spots of color—lime-green flares, like St. Patrick's Day fireworks. His legs buckled, and he fell back against the cage as the Norseman charged forward, bellowing, *"Eyða!"*

Cord managed to duck a hammer-fist meant for the center of his face just as the bell sounded and the ref pulled them apart.

Gears put an ice pack on his neck and screamed at him while he attended to his cuts. "You gotta stuff those goddamn takedowns. Stay off your back. This guy'll kill you on the ground."

Cord pulled in deep draughts of air, closing his eyes, fighting the dizziness, willing himself to find the strength to keep going. Two more rounds, he told himself. Give me two more rounds. He was ahead two rounds to one. That was certain. He opened his eyes, his vision roaming the ceiling and snagging when it reached the clock, which had reset to show five minutes for the fourth round. Next to the timer was an actual clock: *eleven-fifty*. "How's the nose?" he asked.

"It's not great," Gears admitted. He applied a cotton swab soaked in Avitene and epinephrine to a cut above his left eye. "If it gets any worse, the ref might stop the fight."

Cord doubted that. This ref wouldn't stop the mugging of an eighty-year-old lady.

The bell sounded, and Cord got to his feet. Liana's voice reached him from far away, but he couldn't make out what she said.

Cord stalked forward and took a right to the neck, which sent him down. He got up, and for the next five minutes, received a pummeling. A left-right combo doubled him over and the Norseman pounced on him, delivering a rising front kick to the sternum. Cord felt the splintery give of one of his ribs cracking and then the Norseman mounted him, releasing a torrent of blows while Cord struggled to hang on to a sliver of consciousness. The ref hovered over them, looking to stop the fight. *GET UP,* he told himself. He summoned the last of his reserves, tried to roll onto his back, but the Norseman threw his legs over Cord's chest and grabbed for an armbar, yelling: "*Atganga!*"

The crowd was a deafening roar in the background— a sound like a monsoon battering the shore. The spectators wanted blood, disfigurement, and agonizing pain. He could feel the vibration through the canvas like a warm current. Through it all, he heard one voice standing out above the indecipherable rabble: Liana screaming, "Don't give up, Cord! Fight back!"

Cord felt his arm begin to hyperextend at the elbow, a sickening pain in the joint. They'd both been in this position before, under different circumstances. Except this time the Norseman didn't know that Cord had been training the armbar escape ever since Atlantic City, nearly every day since. He turned his thumb into the Norseman's chest and shoved his elbow up—relieving some of the antagonistic force—then hip-rolled away until he found himself kneeling in the Norseman's guard position. He maneuvered to side-control, but the bell rang before he could land a punch.

"Great escape," Gears said in his corner. "But you lost that round. It's winner take all this last round. Don't leave it for the judges—you need to finish."

Cord nodded. He felt finished himself.

The ref leaned into their huddle. "Listen, buddy. Your face looks bad. I'm stopping this fight unless you show me something."

"You're stopping shit," Gears said. "You stop when I throw in the towel or he goes to sleep. That's it!"

"What do you say, buddy?"

"Let me finish," Cord said.

"Your funeral," said the ref.

Cord took deep breaths, his face bleeding from multiple cuts, his cracked rib pulsing, the swollen skin around his eyes crimping his vision. He looked at the clock: *eleven fifty-five*. The bell rang for the final round.

The ref brought them to the center of the cage for a last-round touch of gloves. Cord hesitated, expecting the Norseman to try to dump him to the ground. Instead, he held out his gloves.

Surprised, Cord held out his own, not noticing until it was too late that the Norseman's eyes had changed shape

and color: one was cataract-white, the other black chal-
cedony quartz.

CHAPTER 32

As soon as they touched gloves, the hall beyond the cage faded to reveal an open crimson-colored sky. Bloodstained clouds with rimmed charcoal edges arced by overhead, forced across by a stiff wind not felt inside the cage. There was no sign of land through the cage's iron mesh, no sense of resting on anything solid, just the sudden drop-off over the sides, the view from the edge of a cliff.

Cord backed to his corner, but Gears was gone, the only reminder of his presence a lone ice cube melting on the canvas. Cord shot a wild look over the side and saw a churning chasm far beneath, a gash opened in the side of the world. Smoke rose upward in thick plumes, feeding sulfur and carbon into the dark clouds that fled across the sky.

He staggered back from the edge. The Norseman must've knocked me out, Cord thought. This is my delusion. Any moment I'll wake up lying on the canvas—

"*Fight!*" a voice from behind said.

He whirled. The ref was wearing the same outfit, but his face was disfigured—long scars raking down the sides, as if his skin had been scored by a three-pronged cultivator with razors for spikes. His eyes glowed vermillion, like hot coals, bright enough to cause a glare. Cord had seen those eyes before. Celeste had shown him: the ferryman crossing the Acheron River. He heard a deep-throated laugh, and his eyes were drawn to the far side of the cage where the Norseman stood, banging his gloves together. Only it wasn't the Norseman. He'd grown in proportion, yellow beard now blackened, a long scar running down the curve of his jaw, disappearing into his beard.

Cord pushed forward. The glove would protect him. *It had to.* The Coroner threw out a wide-arcing left hook that Cord side-stepped and countered with one of his own. He used perfect technique and footwork, his arm whistling through the air, the same punch that had ended Mercy's life. Cord's glove connected square with the Coroner's jaw. There came the crunch of shattered bone. *Cord's* bone. It was like hitting a wall. Blinding pain lanced up Cord's wrist, through his elbow, all the way to his shoulder. The demon grinned, undamaged, then hammered him in the chest, knocking him onto his back. Then the Coroner was on top of him, his massive bulk nearly suffocating.

Outside the cage he glimpsed now a crowd of bodies rimming the edge, jockeying for position. There wasn't enough room, and fights broke out, the damned dragging one another down into the screaming pit. CROWD stretched out of sight, a sea of naked pale-gray bodies clambering over each other like ants, gaping holes punched through the flesh where the eyes should have been. The Coroner hammered Cord's body with his fists. Each blow brought a fresh roar from the spectators. In hell, entertainment was at a premium, and this was the main event.

The Coroner didn't seem in any hurry to finish the fight. He raised his arms to the crowd. Cord managed to get to his feet and scramble away. He leaned against the iron mesh, trying to catch his breath. His hand and ribs were broken, his face so battered that swollen folds of flesh protruded like tumors into his field of vision. The Coroner paused, laughing and beckoning him to the center of the octagon. The CROWD was in a frenzy, its hive mind sending out a single deafening pulse: "*Kill him, kill him!*"

Don't give up, his mind screamed. *Live*. His entire life had led to this moment. But he was forced to acknowledge the ultimate irony: Mark was right—everything had been scripted. Free will was a joke told by a hack comedian. A lie whispered to children. Every choice he'd made was simply another turn of a gigantic dial that opened on the scene in front of him.

There was no sense in fighting anymore. How could he fight something as massive as destiny, a machine whose gears eclipsed entire galaxies, whose chains reached through the millennia, intertwined with the be-

ginnings of all life and time? Fighting made no sense—
but he didn't care. He couldn't quit. It just wasn't in him.
He stumbled forward as the Coroner beckoned, as the
CROWD screamed for his blood, now an electric hum
like the sound of the cicadas around Sterling Lake.

"I'm coming," Cord snarled. "You bearded fuck."

He uncorked a haymaker left that sailed wide, and
the Coroner slammed him to the ground, the breath
thrown from his lungs, cracked ribs barking at him to lie
still. He struggled to get up, but the Coroner's weight
pinned him to the canvas. This time, he was not getting
up. The Coroner smashed his fist against his temple. The
cage seemed to breathe, shrinking and expanding in a me-
thodical pulse. Another blow smashed into his jaw. The
edges of his vision darkened. The demon knelt on top of
Cord's body, gnarled fingers squeezing around his throat,
hands garroting the air to his lungs. The demon choked
until Cord went limp. And the CROWD went wild.

CHAPTER 33

I lost it," Cord said, hauling in the line. "So close."
Mercy leaned over the dock, grabbed a hold of the
line, and yanked it out of the water. "It took the bait,
whatever it was."

"Probably a good thing it let go," Cord said. "If I'd
hung on, it would've pulled me down with it."

"I'd have hauled your ass out of there," Mercy said.
"I owe you one. Or two."

"You're just itching to settle that score, aren't you?"

It was humid, like most early mornings on the lake.
And it was dark. Cypress trees grew in the corner where
they fished, matchsticks jutting out of the water, their
branches growing upward into a cone-like flame that
shaded out the sun's canting orange rays. Cord pulled in a
breath of the lake's briny air. There was a tinge of carbon, something Cord had smelled only once out by this
lake. "You smell smoke?"

Mercy sniffed the air, shook his head. He reared back and recast his line into the water, where it plunked twenty yards out.

A mist clung to the water's edge, blanketing every-thing beyond, blurring the tall grass and reeds fencing-in the perimeter. Arrowhead plants cut through the mist, like swords whose bearers remained out of sight. Without a breeze, the lake's surface was mirror-still. Cord gazed into the water, his image—somehow distorted—reflect-ing off the calm surface. Mercy's clear reflection was a statuesque likeness. "Why does—"

"We need to make some tough decisions."

"How do you mean?"

"Like finding a new place to train."

Cord couldn't wrest his gaze from the lake's surface. Now it seemed to glow with a flaring crimson hue, as if someone had anchored strobe lights at the craggy bottom.

"I got something," Mercy said, standing and hauling back on the fly rod while spinning the reel. His line straightened out and disappeared into the water five feet off the dock. Cord watched as Mercy dragged on the line, his muscles straining through his T-shirt, shaved head glistening in the damp air.

"C'mon, Mercy," Cord said. "Haul it in. Don't break the line."

Mercy reared back with an enormous tug. He nearly lost his grip but recovered and began to reel in the fish. Ten feet away. Five.

Cord caught sight of the fish's back in the water, a mottled shade of tawny-brown. "What *is* that?"

Mercy hauled it the rest of the way in, and they saw it wasn't a fish at all. He snorted and let the object clatter to the wooden dock. "Well, isn't that some shit."

Cord picked it up, felt the wax wood surface, now ruined beyond repair. "Jesus. It's my fighting stick." He ran his hand over the spongy wood. "I mean, Bruce Lee's fighting stick."

"It looks like something my dog hauled out of the woods."

"What's it doing in the lake?" Cord looked at the bizarre light coming from the bottom of the lake, but he had trouble focusing.

"Whatever it's doing in there," Mercy said, "it's a little too late to do you any good."

"'I hate it in friends when they come too late to help,'" Cord said.

"Euripides."

Cord cocked an eyebrow. "How did you know?"

"Nothing but time on my hands, brother."

Cord swung the stick through the air. It wasn't pretty, but it still might get the job done.

"You and your quotes," Mercy said. "You're starting to sound like Liana."

"Who?"

"You get brain damaged in that cage? *Liana*. Your girl."

"I can't think straight. It's this lake, isn't it? It does something to your mind."

"Yeah, you don't want to hang out here too long. It messes with you." Mercy looked out over the lake at the mist rolling in. "I never told you this, but remember how I said my mom died?"

"She fell down the stairs, broke her neck."

"She didn't fall," Mercy said. "That bastard pushed her."

Cord was silent.

"When I was a kid, he told me one night when he was drunk. He didn't mean to do it, he said. It just happened, one of those things. He never got caught. And what the hell was I supposed to do? Who would I tell? I was scared shitless of him. He used to beat the hell outta me. Maybe my bedroom was messy, or I forgot to take out the garbage, or he was drunk and wanted to destroy something defenseless. I blamed him for everything. But the beatings gave me something. When he broke my jaw that time, I came back stronger. I started going out of my way to push his buttons, get under his skin. And then there was the time when he finally realized he couldn't break me.

"He came back from the bar late one night. I was lying awake, expecting something—you know that feeling you get sometimes when something's about to go down? I heard him out in the shed, and I knew what he was after. He came in through the front door, yelling something, calling me a good-for-nothing bastard. But I was already out of bed. He charged through my bedroom door and came after me with the bat, but I threw a right cross he wasn't expecting.

"His nose exploded, and he dropped the bat. So I picked that fucker up, swung it, and connected with his balls. Man, you've never seen someone drop so fast. He never said, but I'd be surprised if he didn't rupture something. It was a helluva swing. After that, we both acted like nothing ever happened, never once talked about that night. He never laid a hand on me again. But for me, it didn't end there."

"I know."

"It was something chemical."

"I know all about that." Cord thought of his mother. Barbara, with her plastic emotions, her cored-out husk. The living dead, or the dying living? Did it matter? He wondered if he would find her somewhere out here on this lake. And his father. He wondered what he would say if he saw Stanley.

The silence stretched out, solidified into something palpable between them. Then Mercy broke it. "I set that fire, Cord."

"Vic, don't—"

"I waited until he fell asleep then went upstairs and set it. That's why the flames burned top down. Not because the old man left a cigarette in bed. I took a bunch of sleeping pills, figured I'd never wake up. Or if I did, it'd be in hell. You weren't supposed to save me. I wanted to die."

"I know what you did, Vic. And I know what your father did," Cord said. "I found the note."

"The note burned in that fire."

Cord shook his head. "It fell out of your pocket when I dragged you out of there. I have it in my drawer at home."

Mercy turned toward him. "You knew? And you didn't say anything all those years?"

"What was I going to say?"

Mercy shrugged, looking out onto the surface of the water. "You should've told me."

"I'm not the one you have to answer to, Vic."

The water, drained of its red hue, now seemed a stygian surface of uniform opacity. The lake might've been an onyx gemstone set in a ring the size of the world. What kind of being might wear that ring on its finger? Staring out into the mist, Cord cleared his throat. "Listen, Vic. I want to say thanks."

"For what?"

"For what you tried to do for me in our fight. What you said in the letter you sent with the glove. I remember now. It was about me and Liana."

"Tried to do?" Mercy laughed. "You sound like it didn't work out."

"I'm here, aren't I? In heaven? Or is this hell?"

Vic shook his head. "This ain't heaven or hell. They call it the Fade."

"I know someone who called it that."

"We're meeting halfway, I guess."

"I don't understand."

"You will," Mercy said. "But not now. You have to get back." Mercy smiled. "Take care of yourself, brother." He got up and walked down the pier into the mist.

Cord tried to spring to his feet, but his legs felt like they were tacked to the boards. He gripped the fighting stick. "Vic, wait."

The mist closed in tight, a sphere collapsing on itself. Cord couldn't see ahead more than a few feet. The mist turned into something acrid that burned his lungs with each breath. His muscles spasmed in a coughing fit. He got to his feet, staggering down the length of the pier. It seemed to go on forever. Mist no longer enveloped him— it was smoke. And fire. The feeling of being trapped inside a burning building. The roof creaked above, bowing down and threatening to cave on top of him. The roar of flames dancing at the edges of his periphery, golden orange shapes flitting through the murky haze. He stumbled, picked himself up, tripped over an unseen object, crashed to the ground. He no longer had the strength to rise. His clothes were on fire. His hair, his skin. The smoke invaded his body like an airborne virus, torching the cilia of his lungs and nasal cavities. He inhaled it, swallowed it in great gulps, choked it out only to breathe it back in. Like water in his cells, blood in his veins— now, smoke in his lungs. He suffered a smoker's lifetime of damage—two packs a day for sixty years—in an instant. The last movements he ever thought he would perceive: his fingernails scrabbling for purchase against the rotted floorboards, clutching Bruce Lee's fighting stick as he slipped into unconsciousness.

Hands clasped beneath his body, hauled him up, dragged him along the floor. *Leave me be,* he thought. But still an unseen force dragged him along, hoisted him into the air. The gloom lessened. A light source lay ahead. A window.

Without warning, Cord felt himself being tugged

backward and then driven forward. He screamed, shielding his eyes from the glass, which exploded outward in a jagged shatter. Someone carried him away from the blaze toward the edge of a clearing ringed by a line of old oaks, except the trees were already changing—they didn't look like trees anymore.

CHAPTER 34

C ord opened his eyes.

He was in the floating cage, only it had sunk deeper into the abyss. The chasm thinned into a sliver of light above. CROWD rimmed the edge, clustered like gnats. The Coroner knelt over him, arms raised in triumph, wooly beard dangling down over his blood-streaked lab coat. Cord thrust himself onto his elbows, scrambled backward to the cage, wall-walked to his feet. He still wore Mercy's glove—now whole—and clutched the fighting stick in his good hand. When he looked across the cage, the expression on the Coroner's face was the classic look of surprise: mouth hanging agape, brow clenched in consternation.

"Come on, big boy," Cord said.

The demon clenched his hands, mouth set in a rigid grimace, and powered toward Cord, uncorking a wild right meant to bash his skull. Cord ducked, and the demon's fist found only air. Cord skirted quickly around to the demon's back, launching a side-kick at the back of the exposed knee. Cord winced, expecting his foot to shatter, but instead, the blow staggered the giant. He lumbered backward and fell to one knee. Cord swung the fighting stick in a wide arc, watching as it smashed into the Coroner's temple. A spray of blood misted off his head. The demon howled in pain, his mouth gaping open in surprise.

Cord jumped onto the demon's back. The Coroner waved his arms wildly, trying to shake him loose, but Cord held on, shifting his bodyweight to leverage the demon to his side. Cord then slipped one arm under the demon's chin, tight against the throat, and latched onto the bicep of his other arm. He coiled around the demon like a boa, choking with his right arm and shoving the demon's head forward with the other. Textbook rear-naked choke. In desperation, the Coroner rolled onto his back, slamming Cord to the canvas. Still Cord held on. The demon clawed at his arms, but the movement only made the submission hold sink in deeper. Cord squeezed tighter and tighter, his entire body a rigid mass of tendons and muscles. He gritted his teeth in a grimace that worked its way into a grin. He'd won.

෧෨෧

The ref waved his arm in the air. "That's it. Fight's over!"

Cord heard guttural choking noises. The body in his

arms was limp. He looked up. The crowd roared—the *real* crowd. Everything came rushing back. He let go of the Coroner's throat—but it wasn't the Coroner any longer. It was the Norseman.

Gears ran toward him and hoisted him up into the air. "You did it!"

Cord was too weak to raise his arms. "Where's the stick?" he managed, searching the canvas.

"The what?" Gears said with a laugh.

Cord saw Liana standing by the cage entrance. Their eyes met. She smiled and pointed to the ceiling. He looked. The clock overhead: *twelve-oh-one.*

She met him in the middle of the cage, treading over *Hell* in the *Fight Like Hell* insignia on the canvas. Others stormed into the cage—a ring doctor attending to the unconscious Norseman, a photographer snapping pictures, the promoter blaring into the microphone. "Dean 'Corduroy' Masland is the winner."

Liana reached around to the nape of his neck. "It's gone," she whispered into his ear.

After a while, a newscaster tugged at his shoulder, asking, "How did you manage to sink that choke with a broken hand?"

"I just closed my eyes and held on," Cord said.

CHAPTER 35

April sixteenth, a new day. They drove back to Cord's place. He and Liana drank a couple of beers and watched the sunrise. A few birds trilled in the trees, lonely, unanswered calls. He had a good view of the horizon, where a huge line of fire ringed the earth. Pale orange light melted into the clouds as the sun crested the skyline, coalescing into a fiery pinball slotted between two oaks in the foreground.

Cord leaned back, feeling the sun's warmth on his skin. In a month, it would be time to dig out the twelve-speed, the camping gear, the baseball mitt. But who knew where he'd be in a month.

Things would be changing for him, faster even than the changeover he'd just witnessed from darkness to light.

He heard the crunch of tires on the gravel. He didn't have to look to know whose car it was.

"It's him," Liana said.

Cord dropped his beer and got to his feet. "Go inside," he said, instinctively bracing for the nausea.

"No."

"Please," he said, but she held her ground.

The car door slammed. Mark came up the stone path, panting, shooting a quick glance backward. Cord saw a hulking form—grizzly beard, jagged grin—sitting in the passenger seat. In the backseat sat Jade, eyes wide, her face pressed tight to the glass.

Even with Mark only a few feet away, Cord didn't feel sick. That was over.

"Dean, please. You have to—"

"I don't have to do anything, brother."

Mark adjusted his glasses. He had deep hollows under his eyes, hair slicked with a sheen of sweat.

Despite Cord's injuries, he felt he still looked better than his brother. "I had a feeling you might be stopping by," he said. He was careful not to look Mark in the eye or watch his hands for fear of being hypnotized again.

"I'm in terrible danger," said Mark.

"Really? How so?"

"I've made a serious mistake."

"Tell me about it."

Mark swept a clump of sweaty hair from his forehead. "I only wanted what was best for you, Dean. I wanted to save your soul."

"And how did that work out for you?"

"It was Jade. She went farther than I ever intended."

"Save it, Mark."

"I don't expect you to understand why I did what I did. I only ask for a little compassion."

"Try me later. I'm not feeling real compassionate right now."

"For the sake of my family, Dean, tell me how you did it."

"Did what?"

Mark cleared his throat, threw a glance over his shoulder. "Escaped from *him*."

"You were there, weren't you? Rear naked choke. You can learn it at any gym."

"Dean, look at this." Mark turned and raised the hair off the back of his neck. He had his own expiration date tattooed onto his skin, crisp black lettering, fresh as the day Cord woke with his.

Mark clutched Cord's sleeve. "Jade has one, too. They're both dated next week. For God's sake. We've got two kids, Dean."

"Mark, it's obvious," Cord said. "If the date passes and you're still alive, the curse reverts back to the caster."

"But I'm the caster. Jade and I."

"Exactly. You're fucked."

In the driveway, Cord saw the car door open. The demon stepped out into the daylight and strode up the walk. The Coroner had shirked the lab coat and scrubs and instead wore leather chaps, rawhide boots, and a black biker jacket with silver buckles that jangled as he stalked past.

"Good fight," Cord told the monster.

The demon grabbed Mark by the collar, dragged him

to the BMW, and stuffed him into the passenger seat. He plodded around the front then turned and paused to glare at Cord.

"Let's go inside," Liana whispered.

"Not yet," he said, holding the demon's gaze. For Cord, the stare-down was nothing new. A technique Cord had perfected over the years, facing off against larger opponents.

"See you in fifty years," Cord said. "We'll do it again."

The demon opened the driver's side door and slid behind the wheel. Cord watched as the BMW disappeared behind the evergreen trees.

બ્જ્બ

As soon as Mark's car wheeled away, a Buick Regal pulled up. Gallo got out and sidled toward them on the walk, detective badge catching the dawn's first light.

"Isn't it early to be sleuthing, Detective?"

Gallo glanced at the blushing sky, as if suddenly realizing he'd woken before dawn. "The bad guys get up early, too."

"What can I do for you?"

"Some unfinished business."

Cord held out his hands. "Go ahead. Put on the cuffs. I'm too tired to argue right now."

Gallo shook his head. "Listen, kid. I'm not very good at apologies, so I'll keep it brief. I talked to the promoter again late last night. Seems he recovered a few docu-

ments pertaining to the event. On one of these docu-
ments, a receptionist recorded the name of the person
who called in advance to set up your fight."

"And?"

"It was Vic Mercy. He paid by credit card to guaran-
tee the matchup and gave his phone number, social, everything." Cord followed Gallo's gaze down to the main
road, watching the first of the early commuters heading to
their nine-to-fives. "So, in short, maybe I was wrong."

"Maybe?"

Gallo squinted. "What I don't get is why Mercy had
a hard on for you two fighting each other. Or why he
fought at all, given his condition."

"Wait here." Cord went inside to retrieve the note
Mercy had mailed along with the glove. "I got this in the
mail."

Gallo read the note and sighed. "Okay, no maybe.
This kid really had a death wish, huh?"

"I don't really see it that way, Detective. I knew Vic.
He wanted to live more than anyone."

"Well, you'll be glad to know the Mercy case is officially closed. You won't be seeing my smiling face
around here anymore. Good luck to you, son."

Cord shook hands with the detective.

Then he went to bed and slept for the better part of
two days.

EPILOGUE

Two months later, Cord returned to Pound-for-Pound. He lifted some weights, hit the heavy bag, practiced his footwork in the mirror. It was hard going at first—his injuries were still tender. Soon the sweat began, and his movements came quicker. His sneakers glided across the mat.

In the mirror, he took stock of his new scars, ones that danced with him. He didn't mind. Some people defined themselves in terms of how much pain they could endure, some on how much they could inflict. For Cord it was neither. For him, pain had been and always would be simply a reminder he was alive. Ready to fight.

Not long after, he fought his first professional fight. He was on the undercard of a PPV World Extreme Cage-fighting (WEC) event in Las Vegas. He won in the first round with an overhand right to the temple. In the post-fight interview, he dedicated the win to Victor Mercy—

his best friend. "I wish he could be here to see this," he said into the microphone, making no attempt to stop the flow of tears.

He received both Fight and Knockout of the Night honors, bonuses that totaled fifty thousand dollars and guaranteed him a spot on the main card in six months.

That winter, under the slate-gray skies of a cold January day, he took a shovel with him to the East Lawn plot at Woodside. With the wind at his back, as the first latticework snowflakes hit the frozen ground, he dug Rusty Suggs's grave. It was the last grave he would ever dig.

 handbook

The wedding was the following April. Father Reginald performed the service, but their vows were their own. During the exchange of rings, before she slipped the ring on his finger, she whispered, "You better keep your promise this time."

When Father Reginald pronounced them man and wife, Cord touched the silver bracelet clasped around her wrist. The gathered crowd hooted and whistled as their limo pulled away from the curb.

Two people stood in the crowd, cheering the loudest. Senator, who had quit politics and now preferred to be called by his new name: Angel. He'd gone to work for Celeste at Inamorata, and he was planning on opening his own Tarot-reading shop. And Lovie, who paid for the honeymoon expenses with cash earned from his new job at MetLife.

One weekend that May, Cord and Liana had some time to themselves—a rarity because of his training schedule and sponsor shoots that took him around the country. She ran her own production company, something she'd built from the ground level. Although she'd given up acting, she found that she worked even better behind the camera.

That morning, Cord vowed to do nothing all day that required physical exertion. *Well, maybe one thing,* he thought, gazing at the soft curve of Liana's hips in bed. A slave to morning ritual, he staggered over to the fish tank—still disoriented from sleep—grabbed the fish flakes, and gave the water a healthy sprinkle. "Jesus," he said, staring at the tank. "No."

"What's wrong?"

"It's Lu."

"Oh, no. Are you sure?"

Cord nodded, staring at Lulu's corpse, upside-down, white belly poking through the water's surface.

Liana put her arms around him from behind. "I'm so sorry," she said. "Where should we bury her?"

Cord thought about it. The backyard was a logical choice, but the new terrier they'd just adopted liked to dig holes out there, and he didn't like the idea of her corpse becoming a dog treat. Then he had an idea.

"I don't know exactly where," he said. "But if we start driving, I bet we'll figure it out."

"A road trip?" she said, cracking a smile. "Count me in."

About the Author

Scott McNeight received a BA in English from Marist College before attending Western Connecticut State University, where he graduated with an MFA in Creative and Professional Writing. *Expiration Date* is his first novel, a thesis project awarded Thesis of Distinction in 2012. He lives in New York, teaches creative writing and literature, and is currently at work on the follow-up to *Expiration Date*, the second in a planned series of books called the *Cage-Fighter Series*.

Made in the USA
Middletown, DE
02 May 2019